Twisted
COW TALES

Debby Schoeningh
The Best of The Country Side

Published by The Country Side Press: North Powder, OR 97867
ISBN: 9798671471830

Created in the U.S.A.

Contents

Rural Communication

I'VE RECENTLY DECIDED after talking to neighbors and friends that communication between husband and wife — although seldom discussed — is a growing problem among rural ranching communities.

You know the kind I'm talking about, like when your husband comes running up the lane behind a herd of galloping cattle and yells at you to open the green gate. Looking around, you see that every gate within a four-mile radius is green.

After years of stressing over this situation, I've finally gotten to the point that I just grab the nearest gate and fling it open. After all, action — any kind of action — is better than none, right? It's kind of like a multiple-choice quiz and nine out of ten times it's the wrong gate. I swear my husband carries a game show beeper in his pocket: buzzzzz, you lose. "I'll take blue gates for $100, Mike."

Or what about the dilemma of trying to help your spouse back up a trailer? For some unknown reason God gave men and women a different set of backing-up hand signals. Things always start out smooth, and inevitably fall apart at a rather rapid rate.

I'll be doing what I perceive as an excellent job of trafficking, telling him to go left, then right, then forward, because he went too far right, then left again. This will go on for several minutes while I'm patiently thinking he's bound to get it soon. All of a sudden he slams on the breaks, jumps out of the pickup and says calmly between clenched teeth, "It would help if you would tell me how far right or left I need to go."

O.K. I can do that. Just a couple of feet right, I say, now five feet left, no three feet right no back two and a half, now forward again. This time he jumps out of the pickup and rather than clenching his teeth he smiles so big his eyes disappear and I have to strain to make out his words. He says something like, "I think it would be more helpful if you stood over there," only he throws in a few more adjectives.

So I move to the side a few feet and politely ask, "over here?"

"No," he says. "Back farther… keep going… that's it …a little more… just a little more. O.K. good."

By this time I'm 200 yards away, have waded through a creek and climbed over two fences. I yell, "Are you sure you can see me from clear over here?"

"Yeah, that's perfect," he shouts. "Now I don't have to kink my neck to see you."

At that point, he backs up the trailer and stops within 1/4-inch of where he wants to be, so why does he bother asking for help?

What's even more disturbing than hand signals, though, is the difficulty in communicating when you're standing two feet away and talking directly to each other.

My husband came up to me and asked me the other day, "Can you saddle up your horse and go get a sick cow in?"

"Sure," I respond. "Where is she?"

"She's in the north pasture," he says.

Now keep in mind I am one of those unfortunate souls who was born directionally challenged. So I ask, "Is that the one with the big red pipe?"

"Well, not exactly, it's near that field, but just a little west of it," he says.

"Oh," I say, thinking I understand. "You mean the one closest to the railroad tacks?"

"No," he says. "Down hill from that one."

Pondering this for a minute, I say, "Wouldn't that field actually be up hill?"

Then he looks at me with the big eye-hiding grin and pulls out a piece of paper from his pocket and quietly begins to draw a map. Immediately I understand.

"Well why didn't you say so. That's the one with the ditch

curved like Mickey Mouse ears next to the railroad tracks by the wild rose bushes."

O.K, now that I have that settled, "Which cow is she?" I ask.

He says, "She's the brown one with the crooked neck."

I say, "Oh yeah, she has a white hip and a notch in her ear."

"No," he says. "That's a different one. This one is solid brown."

I ask, "Are you sure she's not more of a red color?"

"Ah, hell," he says. "I guess she's not even brown. In fact, come to think of it, she's not even sick."

There are times though that we communicate beautifully. I can be all the way across the hay field repairing a different section of fence and my husband will hop up and down and flap his arms. To the untrained eye it may appear that he is mimicking a goose with a broken wing, but I know from experience he just wants me to look at him.

Once he has my attention he will proceed through a series of carefully orchestrated movements. For instance, he will walk back and forth rapidly several times, squat on the ground with his arms extended as if he's lifting something heavy, turn his back side to me, slapping it; hit himself on the head and stagger around for a minute, and then walk back and forth again.

I know from these gracefully performed maneuvers he wants me to walk to the pickup, look in the back, get the sledge hammer and bring it to him.

Now that, I understand…

2

Ranch Wives Can't Jump

AFTER MARRYING A rancher and giving up my city life to move to the country 15 years ago, I've had to learn a lot of things about livestock, irrigating, farming, and ranchers in general. Things that someone who grew up on a ranch and takes for granted as being simple can be exceedingly difficult for the city slicker.

For instance, one of the hardest things I had to learn was how to jump off of a hay wagon, out of the back of a pickup bed, off of the back of a 4-wheeler and from the cab of a tractor —all while in transit.

One might ask, "Why would you have to jump off while it's moving, couldn't you just stop?" And, of course, anyone who knows a rancher will answer that question with a resounding "nooooooooooo!"

You see, ranchers can't stop, they can't even slow down because they always have to make good time, and their objective is to finish their chores faster than they did the day before — that's the real challenge in ranching — and most people think it's all about money.

And then there's the added benefit that if they can get their chores done quickly, when they meet the neighbors on the road they can say things like, "See that 400-acre field? I harrowed it in one day. Yessiree, the missus brought my lunch out on the four-wheeler and had the dog steer while she leaped onto the tractor like a flying circus act to deliver my sandwich. I didn't miss a beat, although the wife had a helluva time jumping back on the four-wheeler. The dog couldn't keep it straight — kept veering off looking at gophers.…"

Anyway, if you haven't ever jumped off a moving vehicle, getting the hang of it is a little harder than it looks. The first time I jumped off the hay wagon when we were feeding cattle, I had to run ahead and open a gate so my husband wouldn't have to slow down and I figured that I darn sure better jump far enough away from the wagon that I didn't get run over by the back wheels. So I went to the far side of the wagon, got a run at it, and gracefully catapulted myself about 50 feet into the air and landed smack dab on my behind. If I had aimed a little better I could have cleared the fence and opened the gate from the other side. Needless to say, I couldn't sit down for a week.

On my second attempt, I followed the advice of a seasoned rancher who said to sit down on the very edge of the wagon and just stand up. I remember thinking that it couldn't be that simple, but who was I to question a rancher's wisdom? So I seated myself on the edge on the wagon, but before I had a chance to stand up, the wagon wheel hit a hole and I bounced off like a bag of groceries and once again landed on my backside.

Another well-meaning rancher told me to exit the wagon by stepping backwards off of it. That way, he explained, I would be able to see exactly where I was in relation to the wagon and wouldn't have to worry about it. And he was absolutely right. I got a really close up view of the wagon when I fell on my face trying to step backwards onto the ground.

Realizing that these ranchers meant well, and even followed up by watching from their places with binoculars, I finally decided I would just have to figure it out on my own. Besides, their wives were complaining that their husbands weren't getting much work done with all of the laughing and chortling going on.

So after several more attempts of jumping off at varying distances and speeds, performing knee tucks and nosedives with a half twist, I finally figured it out. The secret is to hit the ground running. I found that if I got my legs moving beforehand at approximately the same speed the wagon is moving and kept them going while jumping, I can hit the ground not only without falling, but I'm already running so it doesn't take as much effort to pass the tractor and make it to open the gate before he gets there.

Catching up to the wagon again after closing the gate takes an entirely different technique though. For several years I tried running and jumping onto the wagon. Sometimes I would make it and other times the only thing I could manage to get my hands on was the bundle of baling twine looped over a post on the wagon. I found that if I spread my feet out about shoulder width apart, I could hang on to the twine and surf across the pasture. Then when the wagon pulled me over a large enough cow pie, I could propel myself into the air with enough momentum to land on the wagon.

But I finally came across an easier way to get back on the wagon. In fact, it was so simple I don't know why I didn't think of it before. Once I jump off the wagon and run around and open the gate and close it behind the tractor, I simply stand with my arms folded across my chest and shoot him a look that says, "If you don't stop and let me back on the wagon you can feed the $$##!!!? cows by yourself and while you're at it plan on making your own dinner and sleeping on the couch." You can say a lot with just a look.

3

Milk Comes From Cows, If You Can Get It

ALL COWS ARE not created equal in a rancher's eyes. There are commercial cows, registered cows, young cows, old cows and all different breeds of cows, which you can pretty much group into one category.

And then there are milk cows....

Now, it's my understanding that all cows give milk, so I was perplexed to find out that while ranchers like cows, they tend to not be very fond of milk cows.

So when I mentioned to several ranchers, including my husband, Mike, of my desire to get a milk cow, most of them gave me that "look." It's the same kind of look you might get if your shopping cart accidentally plowed into their brand new shiny pickup in the grocery store parking lot and left a small, but visible, dent. Somewhere between not very well concealed disappointment and confusion over your stupidity.

But I didn't want just any old milk cow, I explained. I wanted one with big brown eyes with long fluttery eyelashes and a cute face — like the "contented cow" on the Carnation evaporated milk can. Surely that should make a difference?

Mike tried to talk me out of it. "Wouldn't you rather have a nice new car," he says. "How about a Caribbean cruise? Oh, I know, let's build on that family room you've been talking about."

But my mind was made up. "I want a milk cow," I insisted. (Visualize hands on hips, stomping feet here.)

So after several days of "discussing" my "Debra of Storybook Farms complex," he finally saw the error in his thinking (my mom always said I could argue a sharp pencil down to a nub) and agreed to help me find a cow.

We bought her from a dairy and it was love at first sight — my sight anyway. She was a Jersey with big brown eyes, fluttery lashes and the whole cute cow bit. She even had the perfect cute cow name — Bessie. Could it just get any better?

Around 6 a.m. the next morning, before he went to work, Mike gave me instructions on how to milk her, and found me a one-legged milk stool. After about 30 minutes of trying to figure out why it only had one leg and how to balance on it, I concluded that dairy companies must break the other three legs off to deter you from trying to milk a cow yourself and instead buy milk from them.

So after my stint of hopping around the barn on the stool like a kid on a pogo stick, I led Bessie in with a little grain and was ready to let the milking commence. Now, most people, myself included, realize that you don't just set the bucket under the cow and expect the milk to come pouring out, but what you might not realize is that there's more to it than just squeezing — I didn't anyway.

Consequently, I squeezed — nothing happened. I pulled — still nothing happened. I twisted — something happened — she kicked me square in the shin and knocked me off my one-legged stool.

Determined, I got back on the stool and tried again. This time, I remembered what Mike had said about using the thumb and index finger to start squeezing at the top before systematically squeezing with the other three fingers and managed to get some milk. I was so excited! I was actually milking a cow — not just any cow — my cow.

I looked up from the bucket to let out a whoop of triumph and Bessie smacked me right in the face with her wet tail (hopefully I don't have to explain to you why a cow's tail is almost always wet) and knocked me off my stool again.

But I persevered and two hours later, I had managed to get about a half-gallon of milk. The dairy said I could expect about one and a half gallons twice a day, so I knew it wasn't enough, but I decided that it wasn't bad for my first time.

So as I was admiring the creamy white liquid in awe of what

I had just done and rubbing my hands, which were seemingly cramped permanently in the milking position, Bessie stuck her big dirty foot right in the bucket.

"I had plans for that milk," I shouted at her, but she didn't seem to care. Being optimistic by nature, I consoled myself with the fact that I could at least give it to the cats that had been meowing and circling the cow like vultures waiting for road kill ever since I brought her into the barn.

I tried to lift her foot out of the bucket to no avail. In fact, she shifted all of her weight to that single foot in the bucket, balancing herself similarly to my one-legged milk stool. Not to be outdone by a cantankerous old Jersey, I put my backside against her hip that was supporting her, braced my feet on the barn wall and pushed with everything I had. It didn't even faze her. But she did turn, looked me square in the eyes with her big brown orbs and fluttery lashes, mooed a moo of disapproval and shuffled out the door with the bucket still on her foot.

Once she got outside she kicked if off, pausing for a moment to reflect upon the whole milking episode... then she stepped on the bucket, bending it so that one side was completely touching the other. It was no longer a round bucket, but a squashed piece of tin with a handle.

Then I got another one of those dent-in-the-pickup looks, but this time from the cats — like it was my fault they lost the milk that they shouldn't have been getting in the first place!

That night when Mike came in and asked me how the milking went, I tried to sound positive and said, "Great" as I dangled the wad of tin for him to see. Sensing that I was on the verge of tears and that laughing might get him in trouble, he offered to go help me with that night's milking. By then Bessie was so full she was practically squirting it out by herself and Mike got two and a half gallons of milk.

Gradually I learned how to milk and went from calling the cow "you flea-bitten bag of bones" back to her original name of Bessie. I also gained a better understanding of the difference between a "cow" and a "milk cow."

After several years, the excitement of getting up at the crack of dawn and making sure I was home every night by 6 p.m. to milk the cow finally wore off, so I bought three calves and told her to take care of them, which she readily did.

Now that the milk cow business is out of the way, I asked Mike about that Caribbean cruise. It's funny, he doesn't seem to recall anything about a cruise, a new car, or a family room. Go figure.

4
_____

Belly Surfing With Draft Horses

DRAFT HORSES HAVE been used for more than a century to work the fields and to do everything from pulling stumps to raking hay. But few are aware of their ability to provide rides that would rival those of southern California amusement parks.

Our first experience with these "gentle giants" began when my husband, Mike, came walking down the driveway leading two Belgian draft horses behind him like a kid with his new puppies. The huge smile of satisfaction on his face was dampened only by the look of disbelief on mine.

"Aren't they cute?" he asks. I don't know if you could actually describe 2,500-pound animals that are six feet tall at the withers with hooves the size of dinner plates as "cute." But I was willing to give it a try.

He said we really "needed" them to pull our cattle feed-wagon, and although they were well broke, there would be a "brief" training period to get them accustomed to the cattle.

And so the experience began. Mike built a training sled that was heavy enough that most horses would have had a difficult time pulling it, but these weren't most horses. To give you an idea of how the events transpired, we started off calling them their given names, "Bob" and "Doc" but as time wore on we developed other names for them that aren't suitable for publication, but needless to say, better described their personalities.

Mike was filled with excitement the day he decided to take them out for a test run. He asked his dad, Pete, to go along for the ride. Pete has always been a sensible person, so it's hard to say exactly why he threw caution to the wind on this particular day and decided to join Mike. Having been partly responsible for feeding and harnessing the animals during the previous weeks, I got a closeup view of just how strong and large they were and quickly, but graciously, declined the ride — I said, "No way."

Pete stepped onto the training sled trying to be supportive of his son's ranching project. He noted that the horses looked very calm and relaxed. Mike was all smiles, as he proudly said, "Aren't they great? I just can't believe I was able to find this nice of horses around here."

Pete said, "Yeah, they are terrific, Mike," as he sat down on the hay bale, which was strapped to the wagon to use as a seat. "How do you make theses things go?" As it turned out, "go" was the magic word. Upon hearing it, Bob and Doc twitched their ears, and shifted their weight to their hind legs as they reared up slightly and took off from an idle position to a full gallop. It reminded me of a Maserati going from 0 to 60 in less than 10 seconds.

Pete promptly fell over backward and rolled off the sled. He staggered back to the barn while holding his back and muttering under his breath — something about #$!!@# horses...we have a tractor for this...#$!!@# horses...kids!... #$!!@# horses... This was his first and final experience with the draft horses.

Pete and I watched in amazement as the horses continued to drag the sled with Mike still on it at warp speeds through the maze of corrals. Mike struggled to gain control by forcing them into a tight circle. The only problem was that the horses kept up the same speed and the sled was almost flying sideways around the circle. By this time the gravitational force was pulling Mike's face back to his hairline, which made it look like he was smiling — really big. We later learned that he was not smiling, at all.

The fiasco finally ended about an hour later when the horses had nowhere to go but head on into a fence. They slid to an abrupt stop, noses almost touching the top fence rail, doing the reverse — 60 to 0 in less than 10 seconds. The force from the unexpected stop catapulted Mike off the wagon and onto the ground. Of course, he later said he purposely planned on leaping ten feet into the air, clearing the horses backs and landing near their heads so he could grab them quickly — the flip with a half twist, landing face first, was an afterthought.

I've heard that you can learn from others' mistakes, but I must have not been very receptive to that bit of wisdom. Several weeks later, after the first snowfall, Mike said, "I've got them figured out now, let's hook Bob and Doc up to the hay wagon and feed with them this morning." I actually agreed to do it and without the promise of so much as a night out on the town. I missed my opportunity for what I later found out would have been a well-deserved bribe.

Everything was going smoothly, Mike was driving the team and I was on the back of the wagon flaking off baled hay and feeding it to the cattle. It was peaceful without the deafening roar of the tractor that we usually fed with. It reminded me a little of "dashing through the snow in a two-horse hay wagon."

It didn't last long. One of the yearling calves was feeling so good he took off running and bucking and in the process he was loudly releasing a little methane gas into the ozone layer. Having little exposure to cattle in the first place and certainly never having had the opportunity to hear one fart, the horses got scared — and off they went.

The faster the horses ran, the faster the calves chased the wagon that held their breakfast. While Mike was trying to control the runaway horses, I was on the back of the wagon cramming my fingers between the floorboards trying to find a place to hang on.

When it became apparent that I couldn't hold on any longer, I jumped off and landed with my right foot in a gopher hole, twisting my ankle. It wouldn't have been too bad but I also landed right in front of 500 yearling calves that were running right at me in their quest for food. I managed to half crawl and walk to the side of the field, narrowly escaping the trampling hooves.

In the meantime, the horses hit a big hole, which spilled several bales of hay onto the ground for the calves, so they stopped chasing the wagon. But in the process the horses had broken free of the wagon and, Mike not being one to give up easily, was still hanging onto the reins. At this point with no wagon holding them back, the horses were able to increase their speed, which they readily did every time they looked back and saw Mike belly surfing through the snow behind them as he maintained his grip on the reins.

Once in awhile they would slow down enough that Mike could get on his knees, and one time he almost made it to his feet before they looked back and got scared again. Since there wasn't any way I could help, and he was ignoring my pleas for him to let go of the reins, I began judging his snow surfing abilities. I think he could have won something for his one handed roll over with a knee to the chin if this had been an actual competition.

The horses zigzagged across the field for a good 20 minutes before screeching to a halt in a fenced corner of the field. Mike stood up, dug the snow out of his coat and pants and led them back to the barn. This is actually when Bob and Doc began to develop their new names. I suspect he was having a difficult time deciding on which of the long list of names to use that he had given them during his snow-surfing demonstration. In the end, he used them all — several times.

You would think that would be the end of it, but he talked me into feeding with them several times after that — determined to make it work, and he did — occasionally. But we (mainly me) finally tired of the daily race around the field, and Mike couldn't talk anyone else into helping him feed with them, so he eventually sold them to a man who uses them in draft horse pulling competitions. Which, by the way, we found out later was what they were originally trained for — and I hear they are doing quite well.

5

High-Centered On A Fence Pole

IT WAS A beautiful day in the neighborhood, the sun was shinning with nary a cloud in the brilliant blue sky. The birds were singing, the squirrels were playing and I, well… I was sort of stuck on the fence. High-centered, actually, like a pickup with too low of a clearance.

It wasn't something I had planned, I didn't have it listed as number three on my to-do list as in 1) Slop the hogs, 2) Feed the chickens and 3) Watch husband laugh hysterically while I hang by my armpits on the fence. No, it was completely unintentional and executed obviously without any forethought or afterthought, or really any kind of thought at all.

I had gone outside with my husband, Mike, to help mend a fence that the bulls had been rubbing against so hard that their hides were permanently embossed with the swirling pattern of fence pole bark. But then that's what bulls do to kill time in-between escaping, trampling flower gardens, bending gates and making ranchers miserable.

But to give you an idea of what I was up against, the fence is about six feet high and made of wood poles and posts. The lower four feet on one side of the fence is covered with woven wire, wire that is meshed together in such a way that it forms rows of little squares. Squares, I discovered, that are too small to get the toe of your shoe in.

Anyway, after performing my duties as Supply Acquisitions Person (SAP), which means I pack the poles needed to replace the broken ones, I was all set to help Mike.

He always performs the duties of The Power Tool Manager, or "The Man" for short, which basically means he gets to run the cordless power drill. I'm not sure why he gets to have the manager title for just running the drill, and I'm stuck being a SAP.... Well... O.K. — he does do a few other things like hewing out the poles, cutting them off, nailing them up, bending the wires, replacing the clips and assorted other tasks — but being the SAP is really hard work!

So after I laid out all of the poles needed along the length of the fence line, Mike asked me to "hop" over the fence and help him. Now, ordinarily I can climb over a fence with the best of them. After years of practice I've even found ways to topple over a fence without ripping my britches on the barbed wire. But I was on the side of the fence that had the woven wire attached and there were no footholds to climb up on.

Sensing my hesitation, Mike said, "It's easy, just get a run at it and hoist yourself up to the top pole and jump over."

"Okay, here goes," I said as I backed halfway across the field. I hunkered down like a racer on the starting block and took off. By the time I reached the fence I was at full speed, which for me is about the same as a slow jog for most people. I planted my feet and leaped into the air — all the while feeling that victory was mine — and landed on top of the fence pole hooked by my armpits.

Mike, still on the other side of the fence, "leisurely" rushed to my aid. He would have come faster but, as he noted later, it's hard to rush and laugh at the same time.

So there I was dangling like a kitten in a tree and the only thing Mike could think to do between holding his gut and wiping teary eyes was to grab my hands and pull. Well, if you have ever had the misfortune of hanging by your armpits, you'd know that the rest of your body doesn't easily follow your arms over an obstacle. As Mike also later pointed out, the screaming in agony coming from me didn't help the situation much either.

So I summoned up all my strength, which isn't saying much, to try and hoist myself over as I tried to find a foothold. But my feet just kept peeling out on the slick wire as I dangled there helpless.

Apparently not knowing what else to do, Mike decided it would be appropriate to take this opportunity to show me how easily he can jump over the fence. He leaped from side to side doing one arm stands on the top pole and double flips over the fence as he said things like "See how easy it is," "That's all there is too it," "Piece of cake." To make matters worse, our Labrador, Puddin' Head, leaped around on the ground in unison with Mike. Together they looked like the Flying Schoeningh's Circus act. If I hadn't put an end to his nonsense by finally falling on my butt, Mike says he could have gone on for hours.

The only problem was that when I fell I was still on the wrong side of the fence. Not being one to make the same mistake twice, especially in front of The Man, I walked a little ways down the fence line to a pole that had broken and bent the wire up. I laid flat on the ground on my stomach and inched my way under the wire while fending off Puddin' Head's tongue that she was slopping all over my face.

When I got to my feet on the other side, trying to recover my dignity, I brushed off my pants and said, "O.K., now what was it you needed help with?" After getting no response I looked over and Mike was already on the opposite side of the fence heading for the pickup. He looked back over his shoulder and said, "Stop messing around and come back over the fence. It's time for lunch now, we'll finish this later this afternoon."

So I guess I've finally figured out why he's The Man and I'm the SAP.

6

When Iris Eyes Are Smiling

IMAGINE A SEA of pink and white petunias springing from the soil like nature's art, full of vibrant colors and velvety textures perfectly painted against a background of Shasta daisies swaying in the gentle breeze. Behind the daisies a rock wall provides support to the magnificent towering irises with a combination of lavender, white, blue and yellow bearded petals reaching up to luminous skies of blue.

Then picture Puddin' Head, a black Labrador/Lord- only-knows-what retriever, playfully romping through the flower garden plucking up the $3 a bulb irises one by one before they've even had an opportunity to reach the desired state described above, and carrying them off to unknown destinations.

Then add a rancher's wife to the scene, running through the barnyard in the early morning hours in a robe and pink fuzzy slippers chasing a black dog, twirling a bag of bagels overhead like a cowboy with a lasso (the only weapon at her disposal at the time) while her husband, Mike, calls after her from the open house door, "What about breakfast?"

I planted the expensive irises between some other irises that a neighbor had given me for free and Puddin' Head, being a discriminating horticulturist, carefully picked through and selected the expensive ones for this particular adventure.

When I finally caught up with her she spat out the "China Dragon," "Swing Town" and "Engaging Blue" iris varieties preferring the "Home Style" bagels that I had pelted her with.

Although somewhat worse for wear and slobbered on, the irises appeared to be salvageable, unlike my fuzzy slippers that had not survived the trek through the cattle pens unsoiled. I replanted the irises and this time covered them with wire mesh to discourage Puddin' from attempting a repeat of her bulb raid. My carefully planned garden — complete with a map showing where each variety was planted — was no longer neatly in order, but at least the bulbs were back in the ground.

Having taken care of that, I went back in for breakfast, which my husband, not knowing how long my pursuit would last, had finished cooking. Taking advantage of my absence, he slightly rearranged my healthy menu of bagels (which were no longer an option anyway) and fruit, and presented a breakfast of potatoes and eggs slathered in a pound of bacon grease.

Not wanting to disappoint the cook, as he was obviously pleased with his presentation, I sat down to eat the cholesterol-elevating plate of lard, when Mike said with a mischievous grin, "Someone's looking at you."

Sure enough, Puddin' was standing at the sliding glass doors with a mouth full of irises wagging her tail and smiling at me with shining eyes. Sensing my irritation from the string of adjectives that came out of my mouth, Mike, who has been trying to train her to hunt ducks, said I needed to reward her for retrieving. I said, "Why, in case we decide to go iris hunting some day?"

But taking this into consideration, I opened the door and Puddin' came in and dutifully dropped the irises at my feet and sat as Mike had taught her waiting for an encouraging word and a tasty tidbit.

"Well," said my husband, "Give her something to show her what a good dog she is for bringing them to you."

I glanced at my plate of floating grease gravy sitting on the table, but before I could take any longer to consider that possibility, Mike jumped up and said, "You can't feed a dog that junk!"

So he went and got Puddin' a dog biscuit and motioned for me to sit down and eat the "wonderful breakfast that he had cooked for me." Now I may not be the sharpest tool in the shed, but something seemed amiss. Why is it "junk" for her and "wonderful" for me?

But when I sat down and begrudgingly took a bite, the wonderful flavor of long-missed bacon grease hit my taste buds and I no longer cared whether or not it was "junk." I just savored the moment and thanked Puddin' for the iris adventure that led me to a morning of mouth-watering bliss.

7

In Search Of The Elusive Tamarack

WHEN WE CONVERTED our two wood stoves to propane a couple of years ago I thought my wood cutting days were over – no more mess, no more splinters, no more work and no more searching for the perfect tree. In fact I was so excited I did my hallelujah dance. Well actually it's more of a shuffle than a dance...well O.K.... I just sat in a chair, raised my arms and said woohoo! But you get the point; it was a pretty exciting moment.

But alas, as fate would have it, or rather my husband, Mike, would have it, we once again own a wood-burning unit. To be honest, I could probably live without the stove, but Mike says it's the single most important element in "our" lives right now and getting wood for it is nearly a life or death situation because the stove is situated in the hub of our very existence – the place where "it" (I haven't quite figured out what "it" is yet) all happens — his shop.

A rancher's shop is like his sanctuary and next to his power tools, a wood stove that allows you to work in comfort during the winter, is pretty much like the Holy Grail. So you can see how important it is to spend every waking second either scouting the hillsides looking for wood or at least thinking about where you might go to find it.

But it can't be just any kind of wood — even though it has been my experience that any kind of wood burns — it has to be tamarack.

Finding a tamarack when you want one is like trying to find a buck during deer season — they're just nowhere around. Since tamaracks don't have legs, I'm convinced that they bend and duck behind a pine tree when they see you coming.

We probably could have found more of them if it wasn't for not being able to get off of the main road and actually get into the forest, presumably where the trees are. Every time we came to a Forest Service road I would yell, "There's a road, let's go get that tamarack and go home."

So Mike would drive up the road as I excitedly scouted the area for tamaracks and inevitably about 200 yards later we'd run into a big mound of dirt closing the road. And the roads were never closed at the beginning of the road, that would be too easy; instead they pile the dirt up just far enough down the road that you can't see it until it's too late. Two hours and 30 blocked roads later, I started to lose what little enthusiasm that I had mustered up for this adventure.

At about that time Puddin' Head our black lab and official woodcutting dog who sat next to me in the pickup stopped sticking her tongue in my ear and slobbering all over me, and laid down. When she stops being excited, you know it's getting bad.

As we drove around aimlessly on closed roads, I tried to point out to Mike that during a forest fire all of the trees are burned, including the abundant pine, fir and spruce, not just the tamarack. So I told him that I'm pretty sure that they are capable of igniting and burning in a wood stove as well. I even went so far as to suggest that I saw an ad in the newspaper about firewood for sale.

He immediately gave me that look, the look that says, "How dare you even think that I could put just any old pine tree in my shop stove!" Apparently I had lost my senses for a moment and had forgotten the significance of this little outing, we weren't getting wood for just a stove, but "the" stove.

Desperate to find a tamarack so we could get this over with and go home, I started looking on the down side of the hill next to the road… where lo and behold there laid the biggest tamarack I had ever seen. It had apparently fallen over in a storm and had gone unnoticed by previous woodcutters.

"Stop!" I yelled. "There's a big honking tamarack down there."

Mike slammed on the brakes and after a couple of seconds of

careful consideration said, "Yeah, right, I bet it's just another pine tree — you're not going to trick me this time."

"No honest," I insisted, "it's a huge tamarack just laying down there on the ground."

He finally got out and looked, and surmised that I was correct, and yes indeed it was a tamarack. Actually I had no idea what kind of tree it was when I yelled, but I figured it was big and that in itself might be enough to entice him so we could go home and I could get on with more important things.

There was only one problem —the tree lay at the bottom of a steep 30-foot embankment in a little dip, and below that was an even steeper hillside that dropped down into a raging river.

"Oh well, too bad," I said. "Guess we'll have to look for something a little easier."

But it was too late. He had already gotten out the chainsaw and the woodcutting desire was dancing in his eyes.

"Look," he said. "I'll trim the branches and stomp the ground down a little and make a path for you. If you walk sideways at an angle you should be able to make it up the hill with the wood."

It sounded like a good plan and like a sap I fell for it — literally. I took one step down the bank, tripped over a root and fell halfway down the hillside.

"Stop messing around, we have work to do," Mike yelled over his shoulder as he cut the first piece, which immediately rolled down the hill and into the river.

He then decided that I would have to catch the pieces as he cut them to keep them from rolling and then pack them up the hill to the truck. This worked pretty well for awhile until he got about 15 feet down the 100-foot long tree from the top and the width of the pieces started to increase.

I tried packing a few of them up the bank and ended up on my knees rolling them up the hill like a human bulldozer with our faithful dog, not one to miss an opportunity when someone has their hands occupied, began running beside me licking my face and nipping at my heels.

"This just isn't going to work," I protested.

"Sure it is, we can't give up now," said Mike. "Go get me the ax."

So after he cut the pieces and I saved them from rolling down the hill, he split them into two pieces so I could get them up the bank. As Mike worked his way down the tree the pieces continued to increase in size and pretty soon he was having to split them two or three times.

Finally, after about four hours of this routine and as it was nearing dark, we managed to get a truckload.

Like hunters bagging the big one, we were on an adrenaline high all the way home excitedly talking about how we managed to get such a nice big tree, and not just any tree, but the prized tamarack.

I couldn't believe I had balked at the thought of woodcutting again, I told Mike. I said it was so much fun to get out and work this hard and bring home a trophy for all our efforts; it really makes a person feel good. We even made plans to go back the following day and get the rest of the tree.

Once we got home though, it took another hour to unload the monster load of firewood and by the time we showered, ate and got to bed it was almost 11 p.m. We lay in bed for a few moments reminiscing about the day's event, but it took on a decidedly different tone than our previous woodcutting high.

I complained about my back pain. Mike complained about his arms and shoulders hurting from all the wood splitting. I said my legs were already getting sore from all that walking up the hill. Mike said his feet hurt from standing all day. I said my face and ears were chapped from Puddin' licking them so much.

About the time I was trying to figure out how in the world I was going to get out of going after the rest of that tree the next morning, especially after my little spiel about how good it felt to work that hard, Mike turned to me and said, "I bet pine would burn just as well as tamarack, where did you say you saw that ad for firewood for sale?"

8

War Of The Weeds

AS ALL GOOD things must end, the peaceful existence I had with my lawn during the winter months of white fluff, came to a screeching halt when the grass turned green and started to grow this spring. Not that I have a problem with this growing carpet of sod…..it's what happened next.

I awoke the other morning, and as my usual routine dictates, I looked out the window to watch the rising sun. As it came over the mountains and slowly worked its way across the yard revealing the lush green lawn, I noticed something was different. I expected to see a smooth flat sea of green from mowing the lawn the day before. What I saw were little dark clumps that appeared to be strategically placed throughout the yard. I got out my binoculars for a closer look and there they were, like aliens from outer space, trying to take over the grass — DANDELIONS.

It has been said in order to effectively fight your enemy, you must get to know your enemy. With no time to lose I ran to the bookcase and opened up a book on tactical war maneuvers, cleverly disguised as a botanical book on native plants. I learned that Georg Heinrich Weber, a German professor, first classified the dandelion that was brought to the New World by European settlers. And they brought it deliberately!

We can't blame our forefathers for this terrible travesty because the book said the Taraxacum Officinale better known as the Dandelion, Pissabed (because of its diuretic properties), Priest's Crown and Telltime, claimed to be a member of the Composite Family and presented itself as a medicinal plant. The Mohegans and other Indians drank tea made from the leaves and roots to cure ailments, and settlers later introduced it to the

Midwest because of its long blooming season to provide food for the bees.

It's hard to say when this seemingly benign plant turned on us and became our enemy, although I'm suspecting it may have had something to do with its ability to change form and become an intoxicating liquor known as dandelion wine.

Equipped with this knowledge — and territorial by nature — I knew there was little time. If the dandelions are allowed to mature they will turn in to downy white balls and begin their raid from the air. I ran to the garage, still in my flannel nightgown, and surveyed my arsenal.

Knowing the crafty nature of this creature, I decided on a high-powered spray gun attached to an oversized tank of an unknown chemical agent that had been in our garage so long no one remembered what it was. I strapped the contraption to my back and outfitted myself with protective goggles and a gas mask for excessive spray (no sense taking any chances). As a last show of force I attached lawn aerator sandals to my pink fuzzy slippers. I figured not only would they intimidate the enemy, I might as well do some good while I'm out there.

Ready for combat, I stepped onto the lawn like Neil Armstrong beginning his lunar walk.

The dandelions proved to be a worthy adversary. They grew together in clumps circling like wagon trains in a John Wayne movie, protecting the women and children. Their bright yellow flowers would tilt providing an armored shield, reflecting the sun and temporarily blinding me as I spun about dazed and confused spraying everything in sight.

What's worse, my pink fuzzy slippers were covered with yellow stains no doubt attributed to the dandelion's paint bombing abilities. It seemed as though every time I neutralized one of the self-pollinating creatures, it would produce three more to take its place.

At one point my husband yelled from the porch, "Watch out there's one coming at your hind leg." (I made a mental note to get him away from the cattle occasionally.) I quickly whirled around tangling my aerator sandals together and managed to maintain my balance for a split second before falling into an undignified flannel heap on the ground.

Now eyeball to eyeball with the archenemy we carefully scrutinized each other. Poised with my finger on the trigger I took deadly aim with my high-powered weapon and my hand began to tremble. I realized for a brief instant, it's true what they say, never look into the eyes of the enemy or you will loose your ability to shoot him. I dropped my gun and I thought I saw him sigh with relief although it could have been the wind blowing.

Memories began to flood my mind of childhood days when someone would pluck a dandelion and rub it on my chin to see if I liked boys. Although the outcome isn't important at this time, I do believe it's a ritual still practiced today.

And I remembered all of the times my once young son would bring me a dandelion bouquet. Proud of his accomplishment I would put them in a vase, setting them on the dinning room table for all to admire.

It was right then and there I decided to cease and desist all aggressive action against this Priest's Crown, the Telltime, this Pissabed if you will. This once noxious weed suddenly turned into a delicate little flower right before my eyes. As I scanned over the sea of green laced with yellow flowers, I started questioning my previous animosity toward these alien creatures. Peace negotiations began and we reached an amicable agreement — as long as they don't try to completely take over, they can stay.

Although I do lop one's head off with the lawn mower from time to time, I no longer consider the dandelion an archenemy. I am currently devoting my time and energy to the annihilation of another well-known adversary, the Thistle. Once again in referencing my tactical war maneuvers book I find its real name is Cnicus Benedictus. Just as I suspected, a direct descendant of Benedict Arnold, all the time befriending you with its pretty purple flowers and then sticking you when and where you least expect it. The war rages on....

9

'Bubba' The Calf

CALVING SEASON HAS always been one of the most enjoyable times of the year for me, and not just because my husband, Mike, does all of the work. Every year I look forward to having at least one bottle baby and I've never been disappointed.

There's always the young heifer that won't take her calf or the cow that has twins and doesn't have enough milk for two. Once the newborn accepts you as their human parent, they are generally a pleasure to be around. I've always been grateful for this yearly opportunity to raise God's little creatures. Until last year...

His name was Bubba. It was a difficult birth, not for him but for his mother. She was a good cow, still is, but as fate would have it she gave birth to a 105 pound bouncing baby boy. Keeping in mind the average calf weighs around 75 pounds, you can imagine her bewilderment when the stork showed up with this one. As soon as the calf hit the ground he was up and running. Unfortunately, so was the mother — she took one look at Bubba and ran for her life.

Mike tried to go after her to reunite the cow with her precious bundle of joy, thinking surely it was some kind of postpartum phenomenon that could be quickly resolved. As it turns out, it was postpartum fear. She hurdled two fences like an Olympic champion and headed into the next county.

I told Mike not to worry, raising orphaned calves has become my specialty. Thrilled at the first opportunity of the year to bottle feed a calf, I ran to the house to mix the formula. Moments later Mike came in and said in an unusually melodic voice, "The little guy's waiting for you in the barn."

Although Mike's smile was larger than normal and a little bit devious, I didn't really think much about it at the time. I had become accustomed to the half-crazed look that most ranchers wear during calving season due to sleep deprivation. Just the night before I had found him aimlessly wandering around the house at 2 a.m. running into walls like he was on some kind of bumper car amusement ride.

So I began the usual routine, which consisted of a four-hour ordeal of cornering the frightened calf, forcing the bottle in his mouth and trying to teach him to suck on something that must taste and feel like a used tire.

The first two days were typical of how most calves respond so it wasn't until later that I realized the reason for Mike's covert source of amusement. By the third day Bubba had developed a voracious appetite. He knew I was the one with the food and he was going to get as much as he could even if he had to use force. I walked in as usual, closed the door and turned to face him. Bubba ran at me like a bull in a Spanish arena after a red cape.

He knocked me off of my feet and the bottle went flying. He chased the bottle around the barn floor with his nose until he finally realized the bottle was useless without me to hold it.

I had just regained my balance and what was left of my dignity when he came after me again. As he searched for food he began butting my legs with enough intensity that he managed to knock me down a few more times. The ungraceful manner in which the calf catapulted me around the barn left me staggering like the loser on Saturday Night Wrestling. Up until now I had only witnessed this kind of entertainment. I now had the privilege of participating.

By the time I finally got the bottle in his mouth he drank all of the milk down like there was no tomorrow. But Bubba wanted more and he wanted it now.

In an effort to subdue him, I tried a tactic I'd often seen at rodeos in the bulldogging event. I grabbed him around the neck and wrestled him to the ground and promptly sat on him. Before I had a chance to say, "Take that, you ungracious bovine," Bubba somehow managed to fling me face first on the floor. As he stood over me looking like a poster calf for "Got More Milk?" I sensed there was a feeling of superiority coming from him.

Although somewhat unsuccessful, my tackle or his, depending on which way you want to look at it, seemed to calm him a little. I thought the battle was over and as I turned to leave, I seemed to remember a saying about never turning your back on the enemy coming to mind, but for some reason it didn't fully register at the time.

Unfortunately, Bubba wasn't ready to give up. He gathered up some speed for this one and planted his rock hard head firmly on my backside. He got my attention, but not the milk he was looking for—-I made a run for the door. He blocked my every move, when I zigged he counter zagged. Finally I threw the empty bottle across the floor and when he dove after it I made my escape.

Daily food fights with Bubba became an unpleasant ritual four times a day, which began to take its toll. I became, well...let's say mildly annoyed at every new bruise I acquired. I not so lovingly referred to Bubba as the mammoth calf from down under, and I didn't mean Australia.

A short time later a cow had a calf that didn't survive and while Mike was pondering whether or not to try and get her to adopt Bubba, I shoved them into a pen together. I wasn't about to feed this guy any longer than I had to.

The cow was leery of Bubba at first, probably thinking the week-old calf was big enough to be weaned by now. After running in circles trying to get away from him, she finally gave in to Bubba's persistence. Bubba would nurse with such enthusiasm he would literally lift the cow's hind legs off the ground. I suspect she wanted a calf pretty bad, and I wasn't about to convince her otherwise.

This year I gave all of the cows a lecture and told them, "You're the ones who wanted to have a calf in the first place. That makes them your responsibility and you'll have to feed and take care of them yourselves." So far they've listened, but I used the same kind of psychology on Mike when he bought the cows, and you can see how that turned out.

10

Baling Twine 101

WHEN I MARRIED into the ranching industry, one of my first lessons was in baling twine protocol. You might think that baling twine is just something to hold hay together in a bale, and it is, but baling twine is also the cornerstone of all ranching activities. I would venture to say that it's more important than duct tape.

Without it, how would ranchers hold fences together? What else would they tie their stock dogs up with when they won't stop chasing the neighbor's cattle? They wouldn't be able to keep the bumper attached to that old Ford truck without baling twine. And some wouldn't be able to shut a gate, close a door or keep a tractor hood secured in the down position without baling twine.

As you can see, it has a multitude of uses, so it is essential to learn the proper handling of baling twine, and that knowledge has been handed down from generation-to-generation since the days of yore.

History books have revealed that some form of baling twine was used as early as the 1800s. One notable passage was from the book, "Feeding the Cows," written in 1829 by Maken Nominee. In it a farmer reprimanded his son by saying "You pulleth those trousers up with thine bailing twine boy."

Now that I think about it ranchers might be able to make some extra cash by selling baling twine to the plumbing industry for that same use.

The first thing that I learned about baling twine was that it has to be organized — you can't just wad the stuff up and throw it in a big heap — it has to be neatly tied and then thrown in a big heap. You may find yourself wondering why this makes a difference since it all ends up in a pile anyway, but trust me; there is nothing that will get you in more trouble with a rancher than messing with his twine system.

First of all, you have to get the twine off of the bale and there are several things to consider — which side of the bale to cut, where on the twine to make the cut and what implement to cut it with. For this discussion we will consider small two string bales. Trying these techniques with large three and six string bales could cause even more hernias, ruptured discs and greater discomfort than you get with the smaller bales.

Most ranchers use pocketknives or a used sickle blade from a swather, which has been transformed into a cutting tool. However, it is seldom that ranch wives are allowed to use these manly devices so a kitchen steak knife will suffice. (Helpful Hint: Ranchers will usually allow you to use their sharp shovel to cut the twine, but only if you promise to dig a couple of postholes with it when you are done.)

Once you have selected a cutting tool, the bales must be rotated so that the knots tied by the baling machine are on top of the bale. Now for the incision, the twine must be cut exactly 1/2 inch in front of the knot. Cutting too close to the knot or too far from the knot could cause the demise of the ranching industry as we know it. (Helpful Hint: I got this one from Martha Stewart — Tape a small laminated paper ruler to the side of your steak knife handle — It's a good thing!)

While hand-feeding cattle from the back of a hay wagon, you must learn to juggle several cut strands of twine at once. This is because you are not allowed to put a strand down at anytime during the feeding process. I'm not sure why this is, but I found that doing so causes a rancher to swear, flail his arms and dart around the hay wagon like a chicken with a fox in the henhouse.

On a similar note, you can't tie a few strands together or tie even half of the strands together, you must keep them neatly organized until you are completely finished, whether you have 10 bales with 20 strings or 40 bales with 80 strings, it makes no difference. (Helpful Hint: If you get more strands in your hands than you can manage, try putting some in your mouth, between your knees and under your arm pits.)

However, if at any time you lose a strand of baling twine and it falls off the hay wagon, you must be prepared to lose life and limb to save that twine. Even though they already have a pile the size of Mount Everest in the barn yard, jumping in front of charging bulls to rescue a strand, walking into the middle of a herd of mad cows or even getting into a tug-o-war with a cow that has half swallowed a strand is nothing compared to the ire demonstrated by a rancher when you lose one of his precious stands of twine. (Helpful Hint: Don't lose any twine.)

Once you have finished feeding the cattle, the group of strands are then folded in half, with ends perfectly even (no compromises allowed here) and tied. (Helpful hint: When there are no ranchers looking, you can slip into the barn and stretch your twines out on the floor to make sure both ends are even. To be even more precise you can tack a yardstick down on the floor to measure each strand. Most ranchers won't even notice that you put it there because men are always measuring stuff anyway.)

Tying the twine involves collecting the folded ends into one hand, giving them one twist, (again I'm not sure why, but you don't want to suffer the consequences of not performing this step) wrapping the loop around the strands forming a hole and pulling the loop through the hole and drawing both ends snug.

They are then gingerly carried by the looped end to the heap and flung on top of the decaying pile of twine to be utilized another day.

As you can see there's really nothing to it, but if it seems like it's taking you a long time to learn this ancient art, don't worry, ranchers seem to enjoy telling people what to do.

11

Chicken Poop For The Soles

ALL RANCHERS NEED to have chickens at least once in their lives… in order to appreciate not having them.

My experience with chickens began about ten years ago. It started out with a simple desire to have fresh eggs and turned into a cluckish nightmare.

It took four years of begging to talk my husband, Mike, into letting me have chickens. He had the usual concerns — who was going to take care of them, who was going to take care of them, and then there was the problem of — who was going to take care of them.

Once I convinced him that the chickens would be my responsibility and he wouldn't have to lift a finger, I set him to work building the chicken coop of my dreams.

Wisely deciding to save money, Mike bought an old chicken coop that was in dire need of repair for $50 from our neighbors. He figured we could replace a few old weathered boards here and there and it would be good as new. Five hundred dollars and three weeks later, we had a coop that any rooster and his flock of hens would be proud of.

After I finally got Mike to stop calculating how many eggs it would take to justify the $500 spent, adding in the cost of chicken feed and multiplying it by how many hours he worked, I entered into the world of poultry. I purchased two Barred Rock roosters and 12 young hens and introduced them to their new home — my spotless, freshly painted chicken coop turned into a coop full of chicken poop in about five minutes. No wonder they are called fowl.

Before getting my own chickens, people had told me of the

wonderful benefits of chicken fertilizer for gardens. Now I realize the reason they always tried to talk it up was because they were hoping I would take some of the stuff. What do you do with ten tons of chicken poop?

Before long every square inch of property we had was fertilized with the white essence of chickens and it became harder and harder to think of ways to dispose of it, although we got rid of a lot of it on the soles of our shoes. It got to the point that when we were invited to a potluck dinner, I would take a macaroni salad, baked beans, and a pickup bed full of chicken poop as a hostess gift.

All of that seemed irrelevant though when I went to the chicken house one morning and found the first egg. I was so excited I ran to the house and cooked it for breakfast. Mike and I marveled for hours about how much more yellow the yolk looked and how much better it tasted, but mainly, that if there was only one the next day — who was going to get to eat it.

So began the daily routine of scooping poop and skipping off to the chicken coop with a basket to gather eggs. In the process however, I did make one startling discovery — chickens don't want you to take their eggs. Within a week my hands were completely covered with chicken peck marks. When people would ask about my hands, I wanted desperately to say that I had tangled with a cougar or even a wild barn cat to avoid the disappointed looks that came when I said, "chickens did it."

It then became a challenge to avoid those ferocious pecking, pinching beaks. I tried several things. Welder's gloves were too bulky and I couldn't pick up the eggs. Letting them eat chicken food out of one hand while I tried to snatch the eggs with the other, just proved they were faster than me. And trying to raise them off their nests with a Handyman Jack... well... let's just say chickens fly at your face when they are really mad.

The only thing that did work was taking my dog into the coop as a diversion — the chickens would fly off of their nests and chase the dog out the door, leaving me free to gather the eggs. After two or three times, just when I thought I had it figured out, the dog started mysteriously disappearing every morning and didn't return until noon.

Then one day after searching catalogs for implements used in chicken warfare and ruling out options like a Hazmat suit and a mechanical robot, I got this horrendous itch right in the middle of my back. I reached for this wooden backscratcher that we had with a hand-shaped claw, and an idea hit me. I ran out to the chicken coop to try it out. I found that I could stand two feet away from the chickens, slip the hand end of the scratcher underneath a nesting hen and drag the eggs out from under her into a padded basket. The hens still pecked like crazy, but put dents into the wooden backscratcher instead of me. It worked like a charm.

Gradually the dog started coming around again, we had fresh eggs every morning for breakfast, and after about five years, Mike finally put away his calculator.

But that wasn't the end of the chicken fiasco. One of the roosters unexpectedly died and the remaining rooster, who unaffectionately came to be known as "Rambo the Rooster" took over the hen house. Now that the hen harem was all his, he passionately protected them from any predators or egg thieves such as myself.

For several weeks as he was sizing me up, he strutted around the coop flapping and squawking at me. Then one day, he couldn't take the act of me gathering up his potential offspring any longer, and he snapped. He flew up and attacked my backscratcher, biting, pecking and clawing like a rooster gone bad. We fenced like sword fighters — he with his beak and me with my trusty backscratcher until he broke my scratcher in half. He spat out his half and came at me with an aerial assault. Realizing that I was no match for this savior of poultry, I made a hasty exit.

For days after the battle I avoided the chicken coop for fear of Rambo. I gave myself pep talks to try and work up the nerve to no avail— "it's just a little chicken, it can't hurt you, now go out there and get those eggs." Then one day I realized that if I didn't get the eggs, there would be baby chicks hatching, which meant more chicken poop — that gave me the courage — the fear of more poop.

So I went out to the chicken coop, this time taking a farmwife's weapon – a broom. I originally wanted to take the shotgun but Mike wouldn't let me have it. I put on rubber boots and gloves, rolled up my sleeves, and literally swept the coop clean of chickens including Rambo the Rooster, who was no match for my nylon angled Broommaster. Rambo kept trying to come back in the coop and I kept sweeping him out the door where he landed on his chicken backside until he finally conceded to the power of the broom.

Everyday after that, all I had to do was flash my broom and Rambo would listlessly strut to the corner of the coop and watch me with his beady eyes as I gathered the eggs — with a brand new metal backscratcher.

12

Guide To Sleep-Deprived Ranchers

WHEN SPRING CALVING ranchers are at the peak of their production season with the hairy little fruits of their labor dropping on the ground, they are also at the peak of their sleep deprivation.

During a night of calving season, ranchers will normally get approximately two hours of sleep. They are actually in bed for five hours, but spend three of those hours worrying about the cows even though they just checked them. The only things that will cause a rancher to worry more are water, taxes, and whether or not the teenager shut the gate to the bullpen.

The calving days are usually uneventful with the cows , but the nights are a different story. The calving days are usually uneventful, but the nights are a different stoy cows have been known to actually stand cross-legged all day to avoid shooting out a calf before nightfall. Cows are also good at predicting the weather and if a cow suspects she is about to go into labor and there is a forecast of snow, she will hold off giving birth until there are a good two or three inches of snow on the ground, and then will only consider letting go of her offspring if the wind has picked up to around 40 mph.

Studies have shown that sleep-deprived ranchers are more likely to walk into walls, kiss the dog and pat their spouse on the head, and use hair spray for underarm deodorant than those ranchers who get enough sleep.

So as you can see this is a stressful time, and there are several things to consider when encountering a sleep-deprived rancher.

First, never engage a sleep-deprived rancher in a lengthy conversation, as he will nod off in mid-sentence. Keep your questions in a format that will allow them to answer with a yes, no, or a simple grunt.

Never ask a sleep-deprived rancher how his calving is going. Doing so could raise his blood pressure to dangerous levels. If you should forget this rule, back away slowly. Do not try to change the subject. Your best defense is to leave. He probably won't even notice you have gone for quite some time as he continues his cow tirade.

If you encounter a rancher that has fallen asleep, do not attempt to wake him. I repeat, do not attempt to wake him — this is for your own safety. Waking a sleep-deprived rancher, who has finally managed to catch a few zzzz's is similar to waking a hibernating bear two months early. This rule also applies to veterinarians who are found scattered along the roads asleep in their vehicles. It may be tempting to wake them, but remember this is their only refuge from the sleep-deprived ranchers.

If you have a sleep-deprived rancher living in your home, rearrange all of the furniture during this time so it is flat against the walls. This will avoid having them wake you up by their yelling and cursing in the middle of the night after they have stubbed their toe or banged their hip on obviously what should have "never been in their way in the first place," on their way out to check the cows.

And finally, be patient with sleep-deprived ranchers, calving season only lasts a couple of months and then they will be back to normal — until haying season starts...

13

Branding, The Musical Version

EVERY RANCHER LOOKS forward to calving season, mainly so they can get it over with for the year, and every rancher looks forward to branding time, basically for the same reason.

We recently completed our branding and we're finding that as we get older, help is harder to find. I've ascertained that either it's because we're getting crankier and harder to work with…or we've gone through all of our family and friends over the years and we can no longer convince them that it's "fun." That only seems to work once, and the following year they usually have something more important scheduled to do at that time like replacing their septic tank.

So this year my husband and I worked the cows and branded the calves with the help of our teenage son who so generously offered his assistance (we bribed him by telling him he could drive the four-wheeler and go as fast as he wanted) and my mother who always helps because that's what mothers do.

As I was trying to find a way to describe the day's events, I decided it might best be related in a song and since I'm not a musician or a songwriter, and you can thank your lucky stars that you don't have to hear me sing it, I worked up this little ditty to the tune of "Git Along Little Doggies."

Git Along Little Doggies And Keep Gittin'

> As I was branding one morning cuz I had to,
> I spied a white calf amovin' along.
> His head was thrown back and his eyes were aglarin',
> And as I approached, He was kickin' me strong.

Chorus

Whoop-ee ti-yi-go, git along little doggies,
It's my misfortune and none of your own.
Whoop-ee ti-yi-go, git along little doggies,
I know that Safeway will be your new home.
It's early in spring that we round up the doggies,
We call all the relatives that offered to help out.
When those two show we round up our four-wheelers,
And we chase them doggies and cows all about.

Once we get the little doggies up into the corrals,
We start poking and prodding and moving them in line.
We mark them and brand them and get stepped on and leaked on,
And some of them doggies leave a little poop behind.

(Repeat Chorus)

It's whooping and cursing and pushin' the doggies,
And oh how we wish they would go on their own!
It's whooping and punching, and yelling at each other,
But we know that we will soon all get to go home.

(Repeat Chorus)

As the day wears on we try not to use our smellers,
Cuz the doggies are cute, but they stink like a sewer.
And pretty soon we begin to take on that same awful odor,
By then we were wishing that them doggies were fewer.

(Repeat Chorus)

The cows were nearby just waiting their turn,
We herded them up to be worked in the chute,
They're a little heavier and a lot madder it seems,
We found that out when they stomped on our boot.

(Repeat Chorus)

The days filled with branding are both long and quite hard,

So we like to complain to almost anyone who can hear.
But the nice thing about it that saves us poor ranchers,
Is that branding fortunately only comes once in a year.

(Repeat Chorus)

Some ranch wives, they go help brand just for pleasure,
But that's where they get it most awfully wrong.
They haven't a notion the trouble doggies give them,
When they begin to find out they start singing this song.
    Whoop-ee ti-yi-go, brand your own doggies,
It's been my misfortune to come help you along.
Whoop-ee ti-yi-go, git out of my way,
I'm going to take a bath plumb full of Calgon.

14

Cold Calves And Toilet Paper Blues

SPRING CALVING IS almost over, but it was an eventful one with the two weeks of cold wet weather that we had. Newborn calves can generally stand the cold, but when they are hatched out already wet into the middle of a rainstorm or plopped onto a wet snow bank, they can't get dry and lose their body temperature in no time at all. But fortunately most ranchers are equipped with the IBCU (Intensive Bathroom Calf Unit).

Our IBCU really came in handy this year. Early one morning as I was going through my usual wake-up routine of staring off into space for several minutes while waiting for my brain to become activated, my husband, Mike, came running into the house with a sopping wet calf in his arms. It had been raining most of the night and the poor critter, which had been born about two hours before, was suffering from hypothermia.

I determined this by checking the calf's vital signs — first I gently squeezed his tail and when water leaked out onto the floor, I decided he was too wet for his own good.

Then I checked with the ECT (Emergency Calf Technician, Mike) who brought him in. He reported that this was "one cold calf," which I confirmed by checking his ears (Mike's were cold too) and I said, "Get the calf to IBCU stat!"

As soon as I began prepping the calf for de-hypothermiazation, the ECT came running into IBCU with another calf that appeared to be suffering from the same malady and informed me that he was going out in the field to check for more. Sensing that this situation could easily turn into an epidemic, I relied on the intermom system to call for help — I yelled from the bottom of the stairs to my teenage son, Jake, who has been working with me as a RCA (Reserve Calf Assistant) for several years, "Get out of bed, we have a calf crisis on our hands!"

By the time Jake had stumbled down the stairs in his half-awake mode and we had rushed back to IBCU, Mike had brought in another calf and had taken off to look for more. So Jake and I began working on the three wet ones.

I took an internal temperature reading on the calves, which is a little more accurate than feeling their ears, by poking my index finger in their mouths to see how cold they were. This scientific test indicated that their status had moved up from cold to "really" cold.

We turned up the furnace and put a portable heater in IBCU on high and shut the door creating an incubator environment. Then we began the tedious task of drying them off with towels while simultaneously rubbing them to get their circulation going. A wet calf can sop up more water than a sponge and takes twice as long to dry.

The calves were starting to recover, but the one Jake was working on seemed to be in critical condition and wasn't responding to routine treatment so we had to get out the heavy duty equipment — the good guest towels and the hair blow dryer.

Like a surgical nurse I deftly slapped the supplies into Jake's hand as he alternately used the blow dryer and guest towels making his way around the entire calf. When he finished, he placed a heating pad across the calf's ribs and wrapped him up in blankets.

The other two calves didn't need quite as intensive treatment, but at one point we had two hair dryers, a heating pad and the portable heater going all at the same time, which blew a fuse.

We had to argue about which one of us got to get out of the sweltering hot box that we had created in IBCU and go down to the basement where it was cool to reset the breaker switch on the fuse box. In the end he won, because he's faster than me, bigger than me and was nearest the door.

I always look forward to calving season, not only because it's so precious to see the birth of a new creature, but also because I generally lose about five pounds during these IBCU saunas.

Once we had the calves completely dry and warmed up, they still didn't seem to have much energy and just lay limply on the floor. We decided to go have breakfast and check on them in a little while, hoping that they would still be alive.

Right in the middle of the scrambled eggs we heard an awful commotion of bellowing, thrashing and crashing. We jumped up in mid-bite and ran to IBCU and flung open the door to find the three calves standing up with toilet paper strung all over the room looking at us sheepishly from under blankets, which were still partially hanging from them. One had even managed to get himself wedged behind the toilet and couldn't get out. It was an awful mess, but we were so happy to see that they had recovered, all we could do was laugh.

The laughter didn't last long though when we realized the amount of work ahead of us — unfortunately the calves were not potty trained, even though they were in the right room for this, and the wet toilet paper that they had some how managed to string all over the room, was plastered on the floor and walls and had dried on them from the heat in the room.

We called the ECT to come and take them out to the barn and Jake and I began scrubbing the walls with bleach and repairing the torn wallpaper caused by flailing calf hooves. And as for the good guest towels — don't worry — they're now shop rags.

15

Basics Of Cow-Herding Language

ALHOUGH RANCHERS NORMAILLY blend in well with the rest of the general population, there are times when they stand out because they speak a different language that is not known to anyone but cows. Because of the complexity of the language, it is only used for special occasions such as moving cattle, forcing them down a chute or into a trailer, and you will rarely hear it used outside of these situations.

But, like the magician who is ostracized by other masters of magic for giving away the trade secrets, I too face an uncertain future in the ranching industry by divulging the translation of this unwritten ranchers' lingo. For that reason, to protect my identity I will be using my pen name, "Bic Fine Point," for this story.

Many of you, I'm sure have heard this language while passing a rancher moving cattle down the road and wondered what it meant. Or even if you didn't wonder what it meant, I'm sure you were awestruck by the sound of these mostly one-syllable words.

Each word listed below basically means the same thing when a rancher is speaking to a cow — "move your tail" — but with a slightly different emphasis.

"Yaw" is the starting word and simply means move your tail.

"Hup" means if you don't move your tail, I'm going to get mad.

"Whu" means I'm tired of saying Yaw and Hup.

"Yip" means maybe if I sound like a dog you will move a little faster.

"Git" means I just realized how silly I sound saying Yaw," "Hup," "Whu" and "Yip", so I will resort to a more normal sounding word (Get) even if I don't know how to say it properly.

A few rules to keep in mind: You have to start with Yaw, because it is the hardest to say and after a few miles of repeating "Hup," "Whu," "Yip" and "Git" you'll find that you no longer have the ability to form your mouth in the "Yaw" shape and will have missed the opportunity to say it. Each word is to be repeated several hundred times before moving on to the next. "Git" will also work for your stock dog when he runs in front of the cattle and chases them back in the opposite direction you want them to go.

Each word needs to be said with a certain amount of force and it's best to practice them for several days before actually trying them out on cows. If said incorrectly or too timidly the cows will just turn and laugh at you. (If in doubt about the proper enunciation you can always ask a seasoned rancher to give you cow-herding voice lessons, but be prepared to spend several hours, as he will undoubtedly take this opportunity to tell you everything else he knows about cows as well.)

And finally, warm up your vocal cords by yelling at your spouse, children or whoever else is planning on helping you herd the cows before you begin. This will also help set the mood for the day and give them the extra encouragement they will need to be forceful with the cows.

Another important note for herding cattle is that if you are a rancher's wife, be prepared to sit for long hours at a time blocking intersections while waiting for the herd to be moved by.

On my way to town the other day my good friend Shelly was engaged in this activity when I stopped to visit with her. She, like most all ranch wives, was told to be at this particular intersection at a precise time, not a moment later or it could foul up the entire operation.

Someone less experienced with this road blocking activity would have been there right on time and eagerly watching down the road for cattle, but Shelly and I knew it would be some time before we saw *anything* coming down the road, much less cattle.

Having had years of experience with this, and knowing that waiting for ranchers to bring cattle down the road is similar to waiting for rain in a drought, she was also prepared with a huge cup of coffee and some reading material. You might also want to consider towing along a porta-potty for just such an occasion.

But if your rancher-husband had the foresight to warm up his vocal cords by yelling at you before the cattle herding adventure began, you would have plenty to consider during your long intersection-blocking wait and reading material will not be necessary.

16

Rancher's Ailments

RANCHERS SUFFER COMMON ailments just like the rest of the general population, but there are some that are indigenous to the lifestyle they lead that most city folks don't get exposed to.

Here are just a few of our most common complaints and their causes:

Four-wheeler Thumb — this is characterized by an aching and loss of mobility in the thumb from pressing the gas lever for extended periods of time and is most likely to appear after hours of trying to round up cattle, and typically only happens when you are on the verge of getting the job done. Just when you are about to drive the last of the herd through the gate, the thumb will cramp up, causing you to let go of the gas and lose your momentum while the cows nonchalantly turn and walk in the opposite direction of the gate. If left untreated, Four-wheeler Thumb will rapidly progress to Damn Cowitis where the mouth forms obscene words, which are released at high decibels and aimed directly at cows.

Ditch Water Hands – this is characterized by sore, cracked skin on the hands caused from playing in the water and building dams all day. This is an adult rancher's ailment because children usually grow tired of playing in the water, giving up long before their hands are affected. Ranchers typically don't know when to give up and often continue playing well into the night. Although Ditch Water Hands is not contagious, oddly enough the wife usually develops Throw The Dinner Out The Dooritis as a result of the cause of this ailment.

Swather Snout – this is characterized by intense itching of the nose and prolonged sneezing caused from removing hay that is plugging up the swather header. As the hay is pulled out of the header, it releases a large cloud of grass pollen that is sucked up the unsuspecting rancher's nose. The pollen that doesn't get sucked up the nose lands on the face and hands and is consequently smeared into the eyes as the rancher feverishly rubs his nose. As in the case with Four-wheeler Thumb, this too often progresses to Damn Cowitis and can lead to another well-known ranching malady, Let Them Starveitis.

Baler Whiplash – this is characterized by stiffness and tenderness in the neck and upper back caused by the constant jerking motion of the baler as it works to spit out completed bales of hay. Ranchers will usually spread this contagious ailment by talking the wife into baling halfway through the field. Once the baling is done for the day, the husband will seek relief by asking the wife, who now also has baler whiplash, for a back rub. When she refuses because of her own debilitating symptoms, the tension causes increased back and neck pain for both and often leads to Damn Wifeitis and Insensitive Husbanditis.

Pre and Post Branding Syndrome (PBS) – this is characterized by intense crankiness and mood swings at calf branding time and both the rancher and wife are affected. It is caused by the inability of the wife to read her husband's mind and know exactly where she is supposed to be and what she is supposed to be doing at all times. Some of the symptoms include unprovoked yelling at the wife like, "Why the !@$&! did you let that son of a $@#$! heifer in the pen with the $#@#!$ bulls? Now we have to start sorting them $$!!##&s all over again!" The wife in turn contracts Stomp Back To The Houseitis and the husband eventually winds up with a heaping case of Guiltitis.

Although the medical field has tried unsuccessfully to find cures for these ailments, most ranchers and their wives suffer along and find momentary relief in Whineitis, complaining to anyone who will listen.

17

From Whence Milk Comes

I WAS IN the grocery store and watched as a little boy climbed up the side of a shopping cart his mother was pushing so he could examine the loot it contained. In a singsong voice he named off the items, especially the ones he had an interest in, "Cocoa Puffs, Pudding Pops, tater chips…" And out of all of the things in the cart, there was one item that he wanted to know where it came from. He didn't want to know how crispy balls of chocolate cereal were formed or how pudding could get on a stick; he wanted to know specifically where milk comes from.

The mother, not missing a beat, quickly responded as she threw a sack of artichokes in the cart and pointed in a far off direction saying, "It comes from over there in the dairy case." Completely satisfied with her answer the boy went back to the task at hand, "pasghetti, hangaburger…."

This little incident got me to thinking that maybe there are a lot of folks out there who think milk originates in the supermarket and are unaware of the role cows play in producing their dairy products. I also realized that cows very seldom get the recognition they deserve for performing this invaluable service.

So without further adieu, here is a list of popular dairy products and where they originate:

- Buttermilk – comes from cows that are constantly moving, churning and shaking their moo thing.
- 2 percent milk – comes from cows that aren't giving their "all" (100 percent).

- 1 percent milk – comes from cows that aren't giving diddley squat.
- Fat Free Milk – comes from health conscious cows that watch their cholesterol.
- Sour Cream – comes from cows that have gone bad.
- Powdered Milk – comes from cows raised in the desert.
- Lactose Free Milk – comes from cows that don't have any toes.
- Evaporated Milk – comes from cows that can't figure out where the milk went.
- Chocolate Milk – comes from cows that are fed a diet rich in Hershey's Syrup.
- Aged Cheese – comes from elderly cows.
- Blue Cheese – comes from depressed cows that are not content.
- Half and Half – comes from cows that give half of the milk to the farmer and keep half of it for themselves.
- Whipping Cream – comes from cows with disciplinary problems.
- Ice Cream – comes from cows when the weather dips below 10 degrees.
- Enriched Milk – comes from cows owned by wealthy ranchers.
- Milk Duds – come from non-producing cows.

So next time someone asks you where milk comes from you can tell them not only where it comes from, but which cows produce the various products.

The next time I went to the grocery store, I tried explaining all of this to another little boy and he just gave me a puzzled look and began to get upset and yell for his mother. So I finally conceded and told him that it comes from the refrigerator, and he seemed perfectly satisfied with that.

18

'Uneasy Rider' Live On The Outdoor Channel

I LIKE TO ride motorcycles. There — I said it. I know ranchers are suppose to like riding horses, but I prefer the two-wheeled models that go when I say go and stop when I put on the brakes. A motorcycle won't turn around and bite you when you're not looking or kick you in the shins when you accidentally touch them the wrong way. And it won't leave piles of poo for you to step in.

Even though motorcycles are great to ride on the ranch herding cows and doing chores, they are also a lot of fun to ride in the mountains. So, whenever I get an opportunity I jump on my trusty mechanical steed and ride like the wind — or at least like a gentle breeze.

A couple of weeks ago I had such an opportunity when my husband, Mike, had to go to the mountains to check some irrigation ditches. We loaded up the four-wheeler and my motorcycle in the back of the pickup and drove to the area where the ditch trail begins, which also happens to be a small camping area where a group of people were staying.

I hadn't been on my motorcycle in awhile and was feeling a little excited and over-confident, so I thought I would put on a good show for the campers who were all standing around their campfire drinking beer and noshing on what appeared to be pork rinds.

After unloading them, I jumped on, kick-started it like a pro and revved all 100ccs. The campers seemed duly impressed...a 100cc sounds a lot bigger than it really is and I'm sure they were wondering how I could possibly handle all that power — and I was about to show them.

So I took off going from zero to 10 mph in oh…I'd say about two minutes, with all eyes on me. I zoomed up the trail, wind blowing in my hair and bugs hitting my teeth, yes bugs can hit your teeth at 10 mph, especially the slow ones, and I rounded the first corner, which converges on a little foot bridge over the ditch. I was going so "fast," I wasn't able to straighten my front wheel out in time before it hit the bridge, which has a three-inch raised wooden edge that sticks up about two inches. The tire caught that edge, and the cycle went totally out of control flipping me over sideways.

I looked over at my now entranced audience and they stood and watched as I struggled to get out from under the bike and pick it up. A 100cc bike isn't that big, but it weighs more than I do so it was a chore for me to pick up. After contorting my body into inhuman-like positions, much like playing a game of Twister, I finally managed to get it upright. I hopped on hoping for a quick exit from this embarrassing situation and kicked the starter and nothing happened. I tried a few more times and still nothing happened.

By this time the campers had pulled up stools and were all seated in a semi-circle to get the best viewpoint. It was then I realized that after having spent the night in the woods, these poor people had gone an entire 24 hours without television and I was like the outdoor movie channel.

Not wanting them to think I didn't know what I was doing, I started fiddling with the choke and various other hoses and greasy gadgets. At one point I even dug a screwdriver out of the attached tool bag and poked it around a little just to show them that I was not completely without mechanical skills.

In the meantime Mike, who was about two miles ahead of me before he finally realized I hadn't brought up the rear, came back looking for me. As he pulled up, I was still poking around with the screwdriver and seriously considering getting out the hammer when he said, "What are you doing? Stop playing around, we've got work to do."

"It won't start," I said.

"And you think poking the gas cap with a screwdriver is going to help?" he asked.

Not wanting to lose my credibility with my audience I said, "I'm checking the molecular activity of the gaseous fumes for conductivity to the transmission thereby establishing a solid contact with the errrr ahhh… catalytic converter!"

He just gave me a long sideways look, carefully considered the source of that string of gibberish for a moment, and weighed his next sentence against his desire to sleep on the couch that night. Then he said, "Here let me try." He climbed on kicked it once and it started right up.

"It was just flooded," he said. "What did you do dump it or something?" he asked half kidding.

I just gave him an airy laugh that may have in some way shape or form led him to believe that he was so far off base that it was funny — it obviously wasn't my intent though — I would have told him what really happened had he taken the time to question me for at least 10 minutes.

So once again I took off, this time a little more carefully from zero to about 6 mph in less than three minutes. I got a little ways down the trail and looked back at the campers who nonchalantly stood up, shrugged and once again began drinking beer and noshing pork rinds as if to say, "Nothing here to see folks, it's all over, move along."

But I didn't just leave them high and dry; I ended up providing them with more entertainment later on. Once we had gone several miles we reached a point where the ditch trail became too narrow for the four-wheeler to continue. So I took the 4-wheeler and headed back to the main road and Mike continued on the cycle. I was to get the pickup and meet him on the other side of the nearby reservoir.

It seemed like a perfectly fine plan until I got about halfway to the pickup and realized that I had never loaded a four-wheeler into the back of anything before. But how hard could it be?

Once at the pickup I pulled the ramp out and placed one end on the ground and the other on the tailgate. It's a one-ton pickup and about three feet off the ground, so the ramp wasn't as horizontal as I would have liked, but I jumped on the four-wheeler and proceeded to climb up the ramp – several times. Every time I would get the front wheels on the ramp, it would flip up on one side and appear unsteady. So I backed up several times and tried to line the four-wheeler up better, but it didn't seem to help.

By this time my audience had turned their chairs to watch this HBO special and I was getting quite exasperated. I finally decided the worst that could happen if the ramp didn't stay in place was that the four-wheeler would simply fall down to the ground, so I mustered up my courage and gave it some gas. I kept climbing up the ramp even though it seemed wobbly and unstable until I finally made it into the back of the pickup. I now know that feeling of conquering a seemingly insurmountable challenge that mountain climbers have when they reach the top of Mount Everest. If I had a flag, I would have placed it in the fender well of the pickup.

Now all that was left was to get in the pickup and drive to our rendezvous point. I jumped in, turned the ignition….and nothing happened. I tried again and again and still nothing happened. The campers were obviously intrigued by this new turn of events because they had moved their movie seats a little closer. They were also beginning to get audio as I spouted words of "encouragement" to the piece of @!#$ pickup.

I decided poking around with a screwdriver this time wouldn't do any good and contemplated asking one of the campers for help, but they were pretty content to just watch. So I decided my only recourse was to get back on the four-wheeler and drive all the way to the backside of the reservoir on it. It wouldn't have bothered me so bad, but the thought of backing the four-wheeler out of the pickup wasn't something I was looking forward to. I reasoned that if it was so hard to get it in there, getting it out would really be a booger.

So I finally decided I had no other options and reluctantly pulled the pickup keys out of the ignition and as I opened the door I happened to glance down at the floor. Wait, what's this? There's an extra pedal down there... Now, in my defense, my pickup is an automatic and I hardly ever drive Mike's and I did at least remember it was a diesel and to wait for the glow plug to light up every time I tried to start it... although I have no idea what that's for or what good it does, but men in particular seem to think it's pretty darned important.

Not wanting to let my audience know that I forgot to push in the clutch and disappoint them — I'm sure up until this point that they had been pretty amazed by the feats I had accomplished this day — I leaned over and fiddled around under the dash for a few moments as if to "hot wire" the pickup as I've seen actors do on T.V shows before, pushed in the clutch, turned the ignition (glow plug be damned) and fired that baby right up.

As I drove out of the campsite I looked in my rearview mirror and the campers had gone back to standing around the fire and drinking their beer. But I was comforted by the knowledge that I had at least provided entertainment for their otherwise dreary day.

19

Fetching Parts Is For The Dogs

TRACTORS, HAY RAKES, balers, combines, trucks and other types of ranching machines are each made up of hundreds of parts. And somewhere, at some time, there was an unwritten law made that says it is the ranch wife's responsibility to fetch those parts whenever one fails.

Taking into consideration that most of us don't know an alternator from a carburetor, one might wonder why we have been given this obligation. You would think that after sending their wives on dozens of unsuccessful trips to the parts store, husbands would see that there is a problem with this fetching system.

The rancher's logic, though, is that he can teach his dog to retrieve an object that is thrown, so surely a wife that is given a part can go fetch one that looks exactly the same.

But in the ranch wife's defense, the dogs actually have it easier. The object that a dog is asked to retrieve is seldom slathered with grease, dripping with oil and unrecognizable. There are not 14 different places that a dog has to look for an object, and they know the general direction in which it was thrown.

For a dog, retrieving an object is not a half-day event. If he can't find it, a dog gives up in 15 minutes, and the rancher pets the dog's head and says, "That's okay boy, better luck next time." But, if after a couple of hours, the ranch wife returns from town and says she can't find the part, the rancher pats her hand and says, "Don't worry, I can wait until you get back from the big city; it will only take you four or five hours and they'll have the part — you can make me something to eat when you get home."

And for some reason, at this point if a wife begins to complain, ownership of everything on the ranch is magically transferred to her. He says, "I really need this part so I can hook 'your' tractor up to 'your' hay wagon and feed 'your' cows so I can make 'you' some money."

So drunken with the power of ownership and the promise of money, we pick up the greasy blob of cold steel again, and willing to give it another try, ask our husbands, "Where does this part go? What is it called? And do I need to know the make, model and year of the tractor?"

He inevitably replies, "Nah, don't worry about it. People at those parts stores are professionals. One look at that part and they will know exactly what you need. In fact, they don't like it if you give them too much information, makes them look stupid." Which loosely translates into, "I don't feel like looking that stuff up and I don't remember what it's called."

So after the two-hour drive to the city and another hour of trying to locate the part store, which by the way the husband could not remember the name of either. He could only remember that the billboard next to it had a picture of a bikini-clad woman and that there was a Victoria's Secret store across the street. The wife finally finds the store and takes the part up to the counter.

The first words out of the parts store clerk's mouth are, "What is this thing and what make, model and year is the machine it came from?"

Remembering what the husband had said, it becomes obvious the clerk doesn't mind looking stupid. And in turn, we don't win very many IQ points ourselves in the process, while spitting out something like, "Well, I'm not sure... I know it came off of a tractor, I think it was a green one and wherever it goes it apparently needs a lot of grease in order to run correctly. My husband said he needed it to be able to feed my cows, if that helps."

The clerk always gives the wife that "look," which roughly translates into, "He should have sent the dog."

So after another hour of watching the clerk thumb through catalogs of parts and occasionally running to the storeroom to compare it to another part, he presents three possibilities. Having been in this situation many times before, we wisely take all three to avoid having to make a return trip.

Three hours later, you make the two-hour drive home with the parts, which with all of the trouble it took you to get them, are beginning to resemble the Holy Grail. The wife gingerly places them in her husband's hands.

The first words out of his mouth are, "I only needed one, how come you got three? And boy, these things are expensive, I would of jerry-rigged something together and made it work if I would have known they cost this much."

With that he heads for the shop and says, "You start dinner and I'll go install this in *my* tractor, so I can hook up *my* hay wagon to feed *my* cows and make *me* some money."

And once again the power of ownership has shifted...

20

The Diarrhea Debate

RANCHERS HAVE A tendency to think that everyone automatically knows what they are talking about. After all doesn't everyone think in cow terms?

I was in the grocery store the other day and decided to go to the pharmacy section and check out the diarrhea medicine. We had a sick calf at home that just didn't seem to be responding to the standard treatment.

As I was browsing the different types and reading labels trying to figure out the best brand, one of the store pharmacists came over and offered his assistance. I decided to take this opportunity to ask an expert which medicine would be best, or if there was any difference in the brands.

So he said, "Tell me what the symptoms are and perhaps I can tell you which type would work better."

I said, "You know, the usual—severe diarrhea with head hanging to the ground and droopy-eyes."

He asked, "Does he have a fever?"

"Well I didn't want to go to the trouble of taking his temperature, but I would say he does by the looks of the blistering on his nose," I said.

"Wow, he must be a pretty sick little fella," he said. "How severe is the diarrhea?"

"Well," I said, "He's pretty much squirting it out all the time, especially when he's out running around through the grass."

"I see," said the pharmacist as he ponders this information for a moment. "But," he said, "Do you think you should be letting him run around outside in the grass when he's so sick?"

"There's not much I can do about that," I said. "He's awfully hard to catch and I certainly don't want him in the house, he's too big and would make too big of a mess."

"How old is he?" asks the pharmacist.

"He's about 4 months old," I replied.

"Good grief," he said, a little annoyed by the sound of the situation. "He's only 4 months old, has severe diarrhea, a fever and you're letting him run around outside in the grass! You need to take him to a doctor right away."

"Look," I said, "we have so many that if I took them to the doctor every time they got sick, we'd go broke. I was just hoping you could tell me what brand and how much to give him. I've been giving him a quarter of a cup of this brand," I said pointing to the pink bottle, "in an electrolyte mix and drenching him with a tube, does that sound about right or do you have any ideas of what might work better? He's not recovering as fast as I would like."

The pharmacist shook his head, picked up a bottle and rather sternly said, "First of all, a 4 month-old should only get 1/2 a teaspoon, if any. He's probably only weighs about 20 pounds doesn't he?"

Not sure what side of the planet this joker was born on, I told him, "I said he was sick, I didn't say he was dead, he weighs about 350 pounds."

"O.K., now I've heard everything," he said. "You're trying to tell me that you have a 4 month-old that weighs 350 pounds!"

"I know, he should weigh a little more than that for his age, but like I've been telling you—he's sick," I said. "He's probably losing somewhere around five pounds a day. He's starting to get pretty dehydrated too. Do you think I should I.V. him with some distilled water and baking soda?"

"This is getting ridiculous," said the pharmacist. "You have a 4-month old son that weighs 350 pounds, runs around in the grass with diarrhea and a fever, you won't let him in the house because he would make too big of a mess and you won't take him to the doctor because you have too many other kids. Furthermore, you are sticking a tube down his throat to give him a gosh-awful amount of medicine! And no, under no circumstances should you attempt to give him an I.V.! Do you have any idea how bad all of this sounds?"

"Well, when you put it like that it does sound pretty bad," I said. "But I don't have a 4 month-old son, I have a 4 month-old calf."

This is one of those defining moments when it took all of my will power not to follow my real teenage son's vocabulary and say "Duuuuuh!"

The pharmacist just shook his head and walked off, muttering something about not being a "dang" veterinarian. As best I could tell our conversation was over and I still didn't find out which diarrhea brand four out of five pharmacists prefer.

21

To Market, To Market To Sell Fat Calves

IT HAS BEEN said that you can always count on two things — death and taxes. For ranchers there are three things — death, taxes and the price of calves will go down the day you sell them. Even if the price has remained at a steady high for three months, the day you pull into the sale yard with a truckload of calves will be the day the market takes a dive.

And to make things worse, the fat little calves that have been at their prime for weeks will go off feed and I suspect take laxatives the day before the sale, resulting in 20-pound loss per head. And those young strong healthy calves that weren't in on the weight-loss plot will act sick in the sale ring with heads hanging low and ears drooping. Some will even fake a limp — you can always spot the fakers — they will get halfway through the ring and change legs, but so subtly that buyers won't notice.

And if that weren't bad enough, the cows add to the pandemonium by running the calves around the fields for hours while you try to herd them into the corrals to take to the sale. This activity results in another 20-pound reduction — both on the calves and us.

The nice gentle cows that would normally walk into the corrals with little or no prompting go ballistic. It's like the minute you step into the field one cow yells, "Run for your lives," and everyone takes off at a gallop. They don't know where they're going — they just go.

And about the time you think you have the herd rounded up and going in the right direction, two or three will bolt and make a run for it and the whole ordeal starts over again.

Now why would the cows do this? We plow through three feet

of snow (up hill) in the winter months with minus 10-degree weather nipping our noses to feed them, and swelter in 100-degree heat, working 15-hour days during the summer months to produce their hay. We care for them when they are sick or in pain. We take care of their babies, if for some reason they choose not to take on this responsibility, and we shell out thousands of dollars for their upkeep and maintenance.

You would think that after all of this, they would be grateful enough to quietly and calmly give up their calves so that we could sell them and get some money for all of our hard work. But nooooooooooooo! They try and hang on to those little buggers until we have to pry them out of their cloven hooves.

The baffling thing is that as I watch the cows out in the pastures this time of year, after months of producing milk for the little suckers, you can tell that they are really tired of them.

The cows actually start exhibiting signs of apathy toward their calves long before the weaning takes place and will no longer even respond to one that is bawling. When the calves were younger, all they had to do was open their mouth and act like they were about to bawl and ten cows would come running to see what was wrong. Now, when a calf bawls, they look around guiltily at each other as if to say, "I'm not going, are you going? No, I'm not going, maybe she will go…"

I've also seen the cows kicking at the calves during feeding time. They try to cover up this activity by acting like they are trying to get at a fly or an itch or coughing at the same time they kick. But once in awhile, you'll see a cow belt a calf square on the head and there was no mistaking her intent. She then looks around to see if anyone was watching, but the other cows purposely turn the other way and act like nothing happened.

Cows that normally wanted their calves by their sides in the earlier weeks are also now sending them off to play in remote corners of the field. Some cows even go so far as to hide from the calves in discreet places such as your flowerbeds and gardens thinking the calves would never look there.

So it's hard to understand why the cows put up such a fuss when it comes time to wean the calves and take them to market.

But I do have a theory — it's not that the cows particularly want them — it's just that they don't want us to have them.

22

Ranchers Are Thankful When...

LIKE OTHERS, WE ranchers like to spend a little time now and then counting our blessings. We have some "different" blessing than perhaps our city counterparts, but nevertheless Ranchers have many things to be thankful for.

Ranchers are thankful when:

- Their $500 stock dog doesn't stand in the gate they are trying to push cattle through.
- The neighbor's prize-winning bull jumps in their pasture with their cows during breeding season and stays a few weeks.
- Nobody notices they are using a little "extra" water during irrigation season.
- They don't make their wives mad enough to leave during the first five minutes of branding calves.
- They can find an irrigation boot for each foot and they don't have any leaks in them.
- They can get a glove out of the dog's mouth that has minimal slobber and few enough holes that it is still usable.
- There are still two or three good posts left in a half-mile section of fence.
- The cows decide to go into the corrals after only three galloping trips around the pasture instead of the customary five.

- They can find the duct tape — because without it, the tractor won't run.
- They have kids old enough to do chores so they don't have to any more.
- They don't get bucked off the four-wheeler as often as they do the horse and the machine seldom turns up lame.
- They finally remember where they put their shovel and it's still there after all those years.
- Someone in town tells them the smell of cow poop on their boots is undetectable even though it can be seen and is leaving a trail.
- They can still use the Come-Along winch to move heavy items when the hitch in their get-along is acting up.
- At least one out of 20 heifers immediately wants its calf and isn't leaping over fences into the next county.
- They look around and realize no one saw their imitation of Captain Hook performed while loading hay on the wagon with the hay hooks.
- They pluck the last of the chicken feathers from between the dog's teeth just before the wife gets home to find out what "really" happened to her Rhode Island Red.

But most of all ranchers are thankful for the opportunity to live and love and share their lives with friends and family in the countryside.

23
_____

It's All About Power...

BUYING PRESENTS FOR a rancher is not much different than buying presents for the general population of men. They basically have the same wants — anything with power: tools, machinery, guns and particularly anything with words like "turbo," "4×4, " "high-speed" or "super size" written on it.

The problem comes in when you decide to try and buy them something that you think they "need" instead of "want."

If the manufacturer of Levis could include something on the jeans' label that said, "Turbo reinforced seams with super size 4×4 seat and high-speed zipper," the gift-giving problem would be solved and wives could finally throw away all of their husband's old worn out jeans.

Or those scuffed up leaky work boots could be easily replaced with a pair of "Rugged 4×4 boots with super size turbo power soles made from an Angus certified steer chased down at 170 mph and shot with a 7mm carbine rifle."

But, since companies haven't utilized that type of marketing strategy yet, resourceful ranch wives have come up with a few ways to sneak in some things that their husbands need while still buying them what they want. When selecting these items pay close attention to the key words written on the box, which will ultimately determine whether or not they will be happy with their gift.

- You can get away with buying a rancher a coat, as long as you accessorize it with a "high speed" cordless power drill.

- You can wrap a scarf and gloves around the legs of a "super size" table saw and use a knit hat as a blade cover.
- A cowboy hat can be concealed as a "turbo" router cover.
- Several pairs of socks can be slipped over the barrel of a "lever action" rifle to protect it from scratches.
- The legs on a pair of jeans can be tied at the ends and filled with "high speed trajectory" 12-gauge shot shells.
- A flannel shirt can be folded and tied as a bow around several "4×4" pieces of "rough cut" lumber.
- Insulated bib overalls can be disguised as a tool apron if you insert items in the pockets such as a "mega" tape measure, "heavy duty" "rip" hammer, "super torque" ratchet set and a "28-inch" "super oscillating" "power grip" chainsaw capable of sawing down trees in a single pass.

The only thing to remember is that a few days after Christmas you have to secretly slip the hats, gloves, coat, jeans, etc. into his closet and dresser without his knowledge, otherwise he will never use them for their intended purpose. And then you have to practice the "look." That would be the dumbfounded look you need to give him when he asks if you know what happened to his router cover, table saw accessories, rifle sleeves, tool apron and shot shell holder.

However, there are some gifts that you can get a rancher year after year because they never grow tired of them, and they can never have too many because they lose or break one a month on the average: livestock whips, hotshots, grease guns, vaccine syringes, fence stretchers, fencing pliers, shovels and pickup tail gates.

And if all else fails, and he doesn't like the selection of gifts you purchased, he can always borrow yours, because it's almost certain that he will buy you that skill saw and shotgun that he claims "you've always wanted."

24

Laughing Cows And Billiard Woes

THE COWS WERE planning something big for Christmas this year. They huddled and chewed their cud for weeks as they discussed what fun antics they could do to make our Christmas more "memorable." At one point I even heard them whispering something about taking off for the next county. From what I could gather they had heard that there was not much snow and cows there still had some good grass available.

Two days before the holiday, they were milling around the pasture behind the house — where we have a large picture window they can see in — firming up their plans. And as they watched us, we could see the excitement in their eyes. They were like youngsters on the first day of summer vacation, bucking and kicking up their heels in anticipation of some serious holiday escapades.

But as they continued to take turns watching us, they began to laugh (as only cows can) and they tee-heed and chortled as they crowed and pushed each other out of the way to get a better view. And the harder they laughed, somehow their plans became less important as they saw how easily we could mess up our own holidays without their help.

We had decided on a family gift this year, or as my husband, Mike, puts it, I had decided and he went along with it because he's such a nice guy. But, in my defense, who would have guessed that a pool table could come "ready to assemble" and be in so many pieces? The sales person said it would arrive in three boxes, one with the legs, one with the top and one with the side rails. So naturally I figured it would be a piece of cake — we'd stand up the legs, slap on the top and attach the rails – how much easier could it be?

As it turns out it could have been a whole helluva lot easier. The "legs" were a pile of boards with bolts, nuts and screws, the slate top came in three pieces with the felt top neatly rolled up and a can of glue beside it, and the rails were in several pieces with the ball holes (or now as bonafide pool experts what we refer to as "billiard pockets") unattached. And if that weren't bad enough, the entire frame had to be built — but of course, all of the parts and instructions needed were included in the handy dandy pool table kit.

Our son, Jake, had gotten a head start on the project by unpacking all of the materials and carefully laying them out around the room like pieces of a giant jigsaw puzzle. After examining all of the parts, we were taken aback at how much needed to be done, but we still figured with three of us, we could complete the project in less than the six hours the manual said it took the "average" person to complete. Well, we learned something very important during the course of the two days it took us to complete it — apparently we're not "average."

We also learned that the instruction manual was not designed for us, the "un-average people," to comprehend. For instance the first problem we encountered was when it instructed us to attach panel number one to the "right side." Well, if you stand at one end of the table, the "right side" is different than if you stand at the other end of the table. So how do you determine which right side is the right, right side?

Fortunately, (depending on which way you look at it) Mike completely took over at this point and began orchestrating the project. He circled the table several times with his trusty tape measure, held up the panel and tried fitting it on both sides, and finally announced as he deftly pulled out his cordless power drill, "This is the 'right side.'" Jake and I were in awe of his uncanny ability to determine which was the correct side, even though it eventually had to be taken down and moved to the "other" right side.

About halfway through the project, and into our second day

of assembly, I was browsing through the vast array of hardware looking for a 3/4-inch hex bolt with a split lock steel washer and a standard coarse-threaded nut, when I discovered a little white box. Instead of just looking inside, of course, I had to hold it up and ask the perplexing question, as most people do, "What's this?"

"I dunno," said Jake. "It came with the pool table kit so it must be something that goes on it." After rotating the little box around and examining all sides of it, looking for writing or other telltale signs of what might be inside, and making several attempts at guessing what it might be, Mike slowly and deliberately said, "Just open the damn box."

Dragging the suspense on just a little bit longer, until I could sense that Mike and Jake were about ready to pummel me with a cue stick, I opened the box...and there inside was the Holy Grail of all pool table kits...the pot of gold at the end of the slate top rainbow...a step-by-step instructional video on how to assemble the pool table. And I had found it. I basked in the glory of the moment...enjoying what it felt like to be a hero and save the day... until Jake said, "Oh yeah, I knew that was in there, I thought you were looking at something else."

After fast forwarding the tape past all of the things we had assembled incorrectly, but were too late to change, we were able to finish the pool table in another six hours. So the instruction book wasn't entirely wrong — after two days of figuring things out and assembling half of the table — it really did only take only six hours to complete.

We had to use this reasoning in order to gain our "average" status again, and show the cows we could do it. Although by this time the cows had tired of laughing and had lost interest about 23 hours earlier — they were off plotting and planning another scheme for New Year's Day.

25

The Horseless Rancher

MOST PEOPLE THINK that if you are a rancher, then you have cows. And if you have cows, then you are a cowboy or a cowgirl. And, if you are a cowboy or a cowgirl, then you most assuredly ride horses.

Well… all cowboys and cowgirls are not created equal. Contrary to popular belief, some of us may know which end of the horse to feed the hay to, but we have never really mastered the art of riding one. And it hasn't been for lack of trying. For the better part of 10 years I rode a horse, his name was "Asbestos." I'm not sure how he got his name; he certainly couldn't be described as hazardous material. But his unusual name did cause some confusion. Whenever the Vet sent us a reminder to get him vaccinated they would say "It's time for Asphalt's booster."

Asbestos was a part of the ranch long before I married into it and belonged to my brother-in-law. He was the oldest horse on the place and couldn't go very fast, except when he got his nose pointed toward the barn and then he'd really take off. Well, really take off for him was more like a child running to the bathroom with his legs clenched. Actually, Asbestos never broke out of trot when I rode him, given a chance we probably could have done quite well with a sulky in the harness races.

He was a good old boy though. When I rode him it was mostly to help gather cattle on the ranch. We usually rode toward the back of the cowherd, bringing up the rear, mainly because we were the rear. Asbestos would have to stop about every two minutes and get a mouthful of grass. If I kept pulling on the reins to keep his head up, he would start stumbling and staggering like he'd had too many fermented dandelions while trying to walk and graze at the same time.

Most of the time it was pretty leisurely work and was performed at this slow pace, but every once in awhile a cow would try to take off from the herd and Asbestos and I would naturally be expected to round it up and get it pointed in the right direction again.

It usually went something like this: My husband would come galloping up beside me and say, "Didn't you see that cow turn back?"

After coming out of my daydream state of wondering if I should wear my hair more like Dale Evans, I would gaze across the pasture and spot the cow and say, "Of course, we were just getting ready to take off after it, but saw you coming and thought we'd better see what you wanted first."

Satisfied, Mike would lope off and resume his place toward the front of the herd. For some reason he always made the mistake of having confidence that this dawdling duo could actually do it. I'm not sure, but it might have had something to do with him wanting dinner that night...

By the time I could get Asbestos to get his head out of the grass and pointed toward the critter in question, it was usually pretty far away. So I'd say, "O.K. buddy it's time to move and this time we have to really go fast." Asbestos would always snort a few times, pass a little gas and start lumbering off in the direction of the cow.

Determined to not let the rest of the crew down, I'd give Asbestos a swift jab in the ribs with my heels and yell "High Ho Asbestos." And after several swift jabs, a few slaps on the behind as well as yelling things that the Lone Ranger would probably not have approved of, he would eventually break out of a race walkers pace and into a trot.

After several more moments of kicking and slapping I would get him into his fastest trotting pace, which by the way for his passenger was similar to riding a foot-high pogo stick on a gravel road – suffice to say anything that could jiggle did with extreme vigor.

It was usually about this time that I would break out into song, a little ditty I made up, which goes like this, "He's the bestos in the westos, my Asbestos." But with all of the jiggling it sounded more like a symphony of frogs with a bad case of the hiccups. Mike overheard me one time and asked if he could get me anything…like a strip of duct tape to block out the offensive noise that seemed to be coming from somewhere in my vicinity…

Anyway, after Asbestos and I would chase the cow all the way back to the pasture she had originally came from without being able to get around her, Mike would come loping up on his horse — performing his eye hiding grin that means he's not really happy with the situation, but, again, he would still like to have dinner that night. In about two minutes he would send the cow flying back toward the herd.

Asbestos and I would soothe our egos by deciding that Mike could have never gotten the cow so quickly if we hadn't followed her into the farthest corner of the pasture through three gates and around two cattle guards and showed him where she was. Then we'd go back to the business at hand of bringing up the rear. The only problem was by this time the rear we were suppose to be bringing up was so far ahead of us that we were more like trackers following signs of fresh cow patties to locate them again.

One day after spending a rather frustrating day of gathering cattle on Asbestos, I told Mike, "This horse doesn't work, I want a new one. Besides gravity is working fast enough on me, I don't need Asbestos to help jiggle everything looser."

By this time Mike had become partial to having dinner so I did get a new horse, several of them in fact, but that's another story…

Asbestos was eventually retired and lived out his last years on the ranch grazing and walking at his own pace, which was usually hard to differentiate from a stand still, but he was happy.

As for me, nowadays when people say, "Oh, you're a rancher, what kind of horse do you ride, is it a gelding or a mare?" I reply, "It's a she and her name is Honda."

"Do you ride western or English?" they ask.

"Mostly vinyl," I say, "unless it's cold then sometimes I will drape an old jacket over her to sit on."

"I see," they say a bit perplexed. "So, you prefer bareback?"

"Heck no," I say. "I ride her fully clothed.'

Trying another strategy they ask, "Well, do you plan on breeding her some day?"

"Nah," I answer. "I may upgrade her to a 150 at some point, but I don't want anything too big or my feet won't be able to touch the ground..."

People don't give up easily though, especially horse people. Even when they eventually figure out you ride a motorcycle instead of a horse, they decide it's because you don't have one, not because you don't want one. That's also about they time they start telling you the cattle working lineage of their mare that's due to foal soon...which by the way they won't be able to keep because they have too many. And since you're a rancher, they will give you a heck of a deal...giddy-up Honda.

26

What Color Is Your Calf Chute?

JUST LIKE OTHER baby animals, calves are cute, fuzzy and cuddly looking. But, unlike other baby animals, they have the misfortune of entering this world through a cow. That in itself wouldn't be bad, but as with all species of offspring, they have a tendency to take after their parents.

Only it's harder with calves because while they are being conniving, obnoxious and just down right ornery like their mothers, you still have the impression that they are just too cute to actually kick you or poop on your boots, so it's always somewhat of a surprise when they do.

I received my fill of the little boogers a couple of weeks ago when we branded and vaccinated them. Of all the jobs available like giving shots, branding, making steers or even just being my husband's "lovely assistant," I chose dancing the little darlings up the bright green calf chute. I thought 'what fun' I'll get to pet them and hug them and squeeze them just like my own little bovine teddy bears.

Turns out they were more like my own little Tasmanian Devils, and guess what? They don't dance up the chute; in fact, they don't even walk up the chute. Heck they don't even crawl up the chute — fact is they don't want nothing to do with the chute and even less to do with me.

I found out on the first group of five calves that I sent up the chute that they have an uncanny ability to turn around in a space smaller than a glove compartment. They all ran up the chute with hardly any prompting or prodding and when the first one reached the head catch, it immediately turned around and the others followed like a cascading Domino design.

Now keeping in mind that the chute is narrow enough that I can't easily turn around in it, I had five calves trying to squeeze back by me to freedom. I couldn't move out of their way, there was no room, and I couldn't make them all turn back around, we were at an impasse. I finally had to jump up on the chute with one leg braced on each side and let them all squirt under me.

It was then I realized I would have to walk each calf up the chute individually, and make sure its head stayed pointed in the right direction. No problem, they're small, they're cute — they're just babies for crying out loud! And pretty soon, I was, crying out loud...

I managed to maneuver one of the calves back into the chute and about halfway to the head catch, he tried to turn back on me. I gently, at arms length, tried to force his head back into the right direction — he quickly rewarded me with a well-placed kick to my shin.

It was then that my husband, Mike, replying to my string of unlady like adjectives said, "Oh yeah, I forgot to tell you that if you stand right against their back end, they won't have enough room to wind up and kick you."

So, heeding his advice, I positioned myself directly behind the calf. He was right, not only was I not getting kicked, I was able to use my legs to help push the calf up the chute. About the time I had the third calf up the chute using this new method, I found out that as with all good ideas, there is usually a little "glitch," and this little "glitch" came in the form of smelly poop all down the front of my jeans. "Oh yeah," Mike said. "I guess I forgot to tell you, they have a tendency to do that."

"O.K. before we go any further," I said, "is there anything else you forgot to tell me?"

"Nah, I think that's about it," he said. "Except the crew is getting a little impatient waiting for you to get the calves up here so we can vaccinate them."

"The crew?" I asked. "Well, you and Mom will just have to wait!" Our "crew" has some how dwindled over the years and we suspect that some of our friends and relatives may have moved out-of-town just to avoid this yearly calf branding ritual. If it weren't for the fact that moms can't say "no" to their children, we wouldn't have any help.

So the battle of the ranch wife vs. the contrary calves continued. As I pushed on their back ends they dug in and braced themselves with their front legs until their rumps went up in the air and I had to maneuver them down the chute like an out-of-control wheelbarrow with no tire. And they continued to bless me with all kinds of offerings — kicks, head butts, toe stomps, half nelsons and anything else they could manage to squirt, wipe or slobber onto me.

Needless to say the calf chute was no longer a bright green and I was no longer in the mood to hug and squeeze the little boogers.

Finally, several hours later, as I was huffing and puffing, bruised and battered, and stuffing the last one up the chute and into the head catch, and pondering a nice long bubble bath, my husband said, "Oh yeah, there is one other thing I forgot to mention."

"What now," I grimaced through unruly strands of hair and a mud (we'll call it "mud" for the sake of decency) caked face.

"The crew is getting hungry — when are you going to make lunch?"

Several time spans came to mind including the one about a hot place freezing over, but I kept them to myself... after all I had to make lunch for mom so she would help again next year.

27

Cows That Go Moo In The Night

TO THE INEXPERIENCED, cows look like mild mannered creatures. While they are scattered throughout the countryside during the daylight hours, quietly grazing in pastures, city folks drive by and say, "Oh, look at the pretty cows. They look so peaceful and content chewing their cuds."

But ranchers know what they are really like. The fact is there is no such thing as a "real" contented cow. The only contented cows are the ones printed on the Carnation evaporated milk can, because they can't kick or charge off of the label. And, if modeled after a real cow, I'm sure the pictures were professionally retouched to "appear" more content.

But when these conniving, controlling, and manipulating she bovines of the udder region really show their true colors is at night. And they become even more colorful during the twilight hours of calving season.

My husband, Mike, and I personally haven't slept more than three hours a night in the past three weeks. Ideally we should be able to go out and check the cows before retiring for the night, get up once in the middle of the night to peek at them, and then check them again in the early morning hours. But it never works out that way.

For instance, just the other night Mike went out and checked the cows before we went bed and came back in and said, "Everyone looks O.K., let's finally get some sleep." The pillows were fluffed, the good nights said and just as we laid our heads down, I heard this soft, faint little noise that sounded suspiciously like a moo.

"Did you hear that?" I said. "Was that a moo?"

We both sat up in bed and strained to listen…everything was quiet. Mike said, "Nah, must be the dog. The cows all look fine tonight, go to sleep."

We lay back down again and almost caught a z when Mike bolted upright in the bed.

"Now I hear the moo too," he said.

Again, we listen closer with the same results – not a sound.

"Well I'm sure it's nothing," I said. "If a cow was having problems, she would really be bawling."

"Yeah, you're right, let's get some sleep," Mike said as he lay down again. This goes on for another 15 minutes until we began to realize what it must feel like to be a windup jack-in-the-box popping up and down while the cow cranked us with her intermittent moos.

But the next time we almost got to sleep and heard a moo, it' wasn't just "a" moo, it was about 20 rather urgent moos in succession, in other words she was "really bawling."

"That's it, someone must be having problems," Mike says as he jumps out of bed and into his Levis. He went out with the four-wheeler and drove through the herd shinning his spot light on each one of the little darlings only to come back and report, "Everyone is fine."

So the next time, about 20 minutes later, she waited until we were completely asleep and started in with the bawling again.

"It sounds like the cow is right under our window," I said. "I'm going to go see what the heck is going on."

So I sneaked out the back door in my terry bathrobe and pink fuzzy slippers trying not to make a sound. Even though it was really dark, I decided not to turn on my flashlight so I could catch the cow in the act and put a stop to this nonsense.

As I was feeling my way through the dark on the outside of the fence that surrounds our house, I couldn't make out the shadow of a cow anywhere. I figured she must have heard me coming and trotted off to join the rest of the heard.

So I stepped out into the pasture a little ways for one last look. Exasperated by not being able to find the troublemaker, I turned to head back to the house, and to my surprise walked smack dab into something big. Startled, I fumbled around and turned on the flashlight, which was pointed straight up between the two of us. When I saw the cow's eerie face in the dark with her black glowing eyes and she saw me (I'm sure it didn't help that I had just gotten out of bed and my hair was sticking up all over) we both screamed and ran in opposite directions.

About that time Mike, hearing the screams, came running out of the house. In my haste to get away from the big black Godzilla cow, I plowed him over.

"What in the heck is going on," he said.

"There's a big black cow out there," I screamed.

Mike, not being one to get overly excited, said, "Yeah, so, there are a lot of big black cows out there."

So I told him the whole "terrifying" story of how I bumped into her and how we saw each other's faces all lit up in the dark. I then demonstrated by turning on the flashlight under my chin.

"Geez," he said as he looked at me in the dark with the flashlight on my face. "That is scary, I better go out and see if the cow's O.K. — you might have sent her into labor.

He's still paying for that one…

28

Every Cowgirl Doesn't Have To Be Horse Girl

JUST TO SET the record straight — Webster's Dictionary defines a rancher as "a person who owns or works on a ranch." Likewise the definition listed for cattleman is "the owner of a cattle ranch; a person who tends cattle." I did notice that cattlewoman is not even mentioned in the dictionary, which makes me wonder if Random House, Webster's publisher, gets a kick back from ranching husbands. There's where those Beef Checkoff dollars really go! But, my point is that nowhere in either definition of the words "rancher" and "cattleman" does it make reference to a horse or someone who rides one.

I mention this because I tried for years to make the horse thing happen, and as my son would say about his efforts to memorize math equations for school tests – it just didn't take!

I tried Missy, a beautiful thoroughbred mare who performed very well – in the corrals. The only problem is once I took her out of the confines of a fenced area into the pasture, apparently she thought she had been set free and forgot all about the passenger on her back. She would take off like a greyhound after a rabbit and no amount of pulling on the reins would encourage her to stop or even slow down until she was good and ready. Fortunately, she had such a smooth gait that I somehow managed to stay on. We sold her soon after buying her, but now that I'm a little older I kind of wish we still had her. She would have offered a good alternative to plastic surgery. The G-force air current caused by her swift ride could be used to pull back and tighten the skin around my eyes.

Then there was Spot, a cute little appaloosa gelding with big gray eyes. He was the perfect size, I could get on him easily and he actually rode pretty nice — that is if I could ever get him saddled! During the brushing, bridling and saddling process he would jump sideways, bite, kick and head butt me to the point that I was so mad by the time I got on him that I didn't want to ride any more. After about a dozen tries and several bruises later Spot became a faint speck in our memories as we sent him back to where we got him.

"Red" was a very attractive gelding, and as the people we bought him from said, "a well-bred ranch horse with lots of experience working cattle," but what they failed to mention is that you needed a seat belt to stay on him. Once he got through bucking and kicking up his heels for the first five minutes you were on him he would settle down and work cattle like a pro. I never did get on him. After watching my husband, Mike, do the bucking bronc bit, I graciously declined as in "Ain't no way I'm getting on that puppy!" He was such a nice horse in all other areas that I toyed briefly with the idea of installing side curtain airbags on my saddle, but I couldn't get my insurance company to cover him for bodily injury (my body) because he wasn't street legal.

Probably the most memorable though was Danny. He was a nice big quarter horse gelding and was actually my husband's horse. Mike had ridden him for several years and had him well trained, but he was still a very energetic horse. This time we approached it from a different perspective and decided Mike would train "me" to ride the horse rather than try to train the horse to "let" me ride it.

To start with Mike taught me how to lunge him in a circle on a long rope attached to his halter. For those of you new to this concept, it involves standing in one spot as a sort of revolving post while the horse goes around and around you going through all of the gaits at your cue — walking, trotting and galloping. Part of the reason for this is to give the horse a chance to warm up and expend some of his initial energy so he won't be overly excited when you get on. This would have worked fine, except going around and around made me really dizzy. Since Danny was well trained to respond to the slightest command, having me standing out in the middle with a whip staggering around like a drunk confused and scared him. He began running forward and back, sideways and up and down.

Mike soon decided that I wasn't doing his horse any favors with the chaotic lunging and announced that he would take care of that from now on and I would ride Danny while he lunged both of us in a circle. Well, the walking and the trotting went fine, but when Mike asked Danny to gallop, things went awry pretty fast. When Danny went from a trot to a gallop it was a bigger transition than I had expected and I fell forward. When I fell forward I did what I thought any sensible person would do — I grabbed around Danny's neck and hung on for dear life.

Although Danny apparently didn't mind having me on his back, he didn't particularly like having me ride his neck so he stared bucking.

"Stop it, you're scaring him," Mike yelled.

"He's scaring me — make *him* stop it," I yelled back as I continued to cling to his neck.

"He's thinks you're some kind of wild animal attacking him, you're going to have to let go of his neck to make him stop," Mike said as he continued to hang on to the lunge line trying to control the bucking horse.

Finally, after what seemed like an eternity, although Mike later said it was only 60 seconds, I mustered the courage to sit up in the saddle and just as Mike said he would, Danny stopped bucking.

"O.K., let's try that again," said Mike, "and this time don't grab his neck."

"Stop the horse," I said through gritted teeth.

"When something like that happens you have just get back on and..."

"Stop the $*!!#%! horse now," I interrupted him.

Mike signaled for Danny to stop, which he immediately did. I dismounted and walked out of the arena on shaky legs, jumped on my Honda and never looked back.

I finally conceded that although I am a "cow" girl, I am not a "horse" girl. My Honda stops when I say whoa, my Honda doesn't bite or kick me, and my Honda only bucks when I ask it to.

And most importantly, my Honda doesn't leave anything for me to step in that I later have to scrape off my boots. "Good girl, Honda."

29

Judging The Miss Heifer Pageant

SELECTING WHICH HEIFER calves to keep and which ones to take to the livestock sale is a big decision every fall, and one that isn't made any easier when the husband and wife make that selection together. I used to let my husband, Mike, pick the heifers out himself, but the last few years I've decided what this chore really needs, is my help. And I'm sure that he will concede that although I may not have the practiced eye that ranchers acquire from years of raising cattle, my help makes for a longer more fulfilling heifer sorting experience.

Our heifer sorting day this week began early in the morning, for some reason ranchers never think of performing tasks in the middle of the afternoon, everything has to take place at sun up like in a John Wayne Western. But, nevertheless, I drug my weary body out of bed and took off on the 4-wheeler with the icy cold, almost winter breeze freezing my lips shut so I could barely talk, much less crack a smile. Hey, come to think of it maybe that has something to do with why ranchers do everything in the early morning especially when their wives are along…

Anyway, I was opening the gates for Mike who was driving the tractor with a load of hay to coax the cows and their offspring into the corrals, when all of the sudden I looked up at the sky and the biggest, brightest moon I had ever seen was resting on top of the mountains, and it was already daylight. Not being one to keep these amazing feats of nature to myself, I jumped off of the 4-wheeler and began pointing at the moon for Mike to see.

He kind of looked from inside the tractor cab in that direction and shrugged his shoulders and kept going. I knew he must not have seen it because he didn't act too excited so I became more insistent with my pointing. Still no response, he just gave me one of those puzzled looks that insinuated I might not be fully awake enough for the day's chore.

So out of desperation to share this beautiful sight, I finally circled my hands above my head into the shape of a big moon and pointed again. This time he looked as though he figured it out. He slammed on the brakes, got out of the tractor and ran over to me and with urgency in his voice said, "What is it, a dead bloated cow?"

"No, it's the moon," I said breaking the ice seal on my lips. "If it were a dead bloated cow I would have made a circle in front of my stomach and puffed my cheeks out like this, geesh! Just look at the moon, isn't it gorgeous?"

With that he shook his head and walking back toward the tractor said, "Let's not make one of your newspaper stories out of this, we just need to get the cows in, get the calves sorted and off to the sale."

Sorry honey, I couldn't help it, I sat down at my computer and the whole "sorted" story just started coming out…

To make this long story shorter, we got the cows in and separated them from their calves, then we separated the good cows from the bad cows, well, let me rephrase that, I'm not sure there is a such thing as a good cow… we separated the cows that were too old, too cranky and too content to produce a calf this year from the rest of the cows.

It's always kind of sad to take cows to the sale, but they always do something to ease your mental pain like kick you on their way into the livestock trailer, which creates another kind of pain that makes you not care so much about the afore mentioned pain.

We took the culled cows to the sale and by then it was time to sort the heifers from the steers, and finally, sort out the individual heifers. So the process began of deciding which cute little heifers get to stay on the ranch, grow up, get fat and turn into demanding, overbearing cows, and which heifers are the go-to-salers. I'm sure there must be a technical name for these, but it escapes me at the moment.

As we sort through the heifers, like judges at the Miss

American Pageant, we quickly get them narrowed down to 12 finalists. Then the real scrutinizing begins to pick out the six best of the 12 best. Unfortunately, they can't parade around in swimsuits or twirl batons while singing the National Anthem so we have to rely on our keen sense of livestock savvy.

"That one has really pretty eyes," I offer. "Why don't we keep her?"

Mike scowls, "What we really need to be looking for is those that have strong straight backs and sound feet. These two need to go," he said while herding them out of the pen.

"Well, none of them are limping and they all have straight backs," I say. "Oh, there's another pretty one. Keep her."

"We don't want ones with heavy muscling, they need to look more feminine," he continues as he separates off two more.

"Like I said, pick the pretty ones!"

"It's not that easy," he said as the Miss Heifer Pageant continues. "We also need to look at their genetics and choose ones that came from higher producing cows. The older ones would also be better because they have a higher chance of conceiving this summer." Then he ushers one more out of the pen to join the go-to-salers.

Now we're down to seven and have one more to go… He scrutinized the heifers from every angle examining their hips and legs, and pondering their mother's history. And finally after 20 or so agonizing minutes he opens the gate and lets one out.

"O.K., that one has a nice straight back, sound legs, she's feminine and her mother is number 57 and she always raises a nice big calf," I said. "So what was wrong with her?"

He scratches his chin and pauses to think, "I didn't like her hair, it was kind of weird looking," he said.

"Like I said, just pick the pretty ones…"

30

Sorting It Out

SORTING CATTLE SEEMS to be an ongoing chore for ranchers. It's kind of like doing dishes, once you think you're done, they somehow get messed up again.

There's always the adventurous (we have other names for this type of cattle, but adventurous will do for now) critter that is constantly getting mixed into a herd where it doesn't belong and no amount of coaxing, herding or cussing will make it come out. So more often than not, you have to bring in the entire herd just to sort out one.

And several times during the year the bulls have to be sorted from the cows, the cows have to be sorted from the calves, the steers have to be sorted from the heifers, the heifers that you want to keep have to be sorted from the heifers that you want to sell and of course the sick have to be sorted from the healthy.

For those of you who are unfamiliar with how the sorting process works, it always involves gates, and there are usually about five different green gates that ranching husbands always refer to individually as "the green gate" no matter which one he's talking about.

Here's a typical scenario: All of the cows and calves are herded from the pastures into a large holding pen near the corrals, which is a major task in itself. Most of the cows have been into the corrals and chutes before and it's almost as hard to get them to enter the holding pen as it is to get a ranching husband to go to the doctor.

Most of you ranch wives have probably experienced this — your husband will run around and around the car avoiding the open door when you try to coax him into going to the doctor, and he will keep bypassing it until you tactically throw a power tool into the seat. Cows are the same way. They will run around and around the pasture bypassing the gate until you throw some alfalfa into the pen or until you make them think they have a good chance of kicking you as they run through the gate.

Anyway, once the cows and calves are in the pen and you've spent another two hours chasing down the lone steer calf that decided to impress his friends by running to the far back corner of the field, you are ready to get started.

Usually it's set up to where the husband is at the beginning of the corral alleyway herding the cattle toward the wife who is in charge of opening the correct gate, each one opening into a pen that will hold either the cows, the heifers, the steers or a sick critter, depending on how you decide to sort.

Ideally, "small" groups of cows and calves will be let into the system of corrals at one time to make the sorting easier. But what usually happens, since the cows are agitated at being in the corrals anyway, they are anxious to get out and will all try to come into the corrals at once.

So as the husband officially announces, "Let the sorting begin," and opens the gate, the cows and calves come running into the corrals and down the alleyway toward the wife similar to the running of the bulls in Pamplona, Spain.

Of course the husband gave the wife explicit instructions before the festivities began of which gates to open and when. So as the cattle come galloping toward her, the husband, trying to sort them as they run in the gate, yells, "Cow, open the green gate; steer, open the green gate; sick one open the other green gate." In a flurry of flying green gates the wife runs from side to side of the alley letting the appropriate cattle into their respective pens.

Ten minutes and 100 brazen cows later as the wife stands in the vacant alleyway panting and out of breath, the husband walks up to examine her work. He looks carefully in each of the pens, each containing a mixture of cows and calves, and declares, "Alright, good job! Now open all of the green gates, let them out and we'll see if we can get it right next time."

"Okay," says the wife. "But could you call them something

besides green gates. It gets a little confusing because, well...I don't know... maybe it's because they're all green!"

Sensing he may be on the verge of losing his free help as well as the prospect of having to eat dinner out, he readily complies and says he will try to better identify which gate he is referring to.

This time as the cattle come running down the alleyway toward the wife again he yells, "Steer, open the green gate that's bent— no, not that gate – the other bent gate, no, the other green gate that's bent on the end, not in the middle..."

Exasperated, the wife yells, "Oh yeah, I see. You mean the other bent green one. They're all green and they're all bent for crying out loud!"

Not knowing what else to do he yells, "Lunch time, honey. How about going back to the house and fixing us something."

To which the wife responds, "Sure, just make sure you don't use the brown door to come into the house. Oh, I forgot, all of the doors are brown, too bad..."

31

The Unsuspecting City Slicker

EVEN AFTER SEVENTEEN years of living on the ranch, I have always been our family's "city slicker." That's why I'm always tickled when I get an opportunity to explain things to other citified folks — like my brother, Tom, for instance.

He lives in the big city area of Portland, Ore., and recently came for a visit. It just so happens that he was here right around the time we normally work our cows and calves. Well, I have to be honest, that's not completely true. We found out he was coming and decided to take advantage of the situation. After all, my mom can't do everything!

We were careful not to tell him of our plans until he arrived and got settled in.

"Oh, by the way," I said casually. "You will need to get up at 5 a.m. tomorrow to help with the cattle." I learned a long time ago not to phrase the job of working cattle into a question such as "Would you like to help us work cattle tomorrow?" That would give unsuspecting relatives the idea that they could say "no" — something we really want to avoid.

"What exactly does it mean 'to help with the cattle'?" he asked.

"Oh, the usual," I said. "You know, giving shots, wormer, applying stuff for lice, etc… nothing too difficult," I assured him.

He shot a puzzled look at Mom who has learned over the years that giving too much information and scaring away any potential help means more work for her. "What does she mean etc.?" he asked.

Mom just shrugged her shoulders and said, "Isn't dinner about ready?"

We managed to keep him occupied the rest of the evening so

he would have little time to think about the events that would take place the next day. And at 5 a.m. the next morning he came bouncing down the stairs ready to go — wearing his crisp white, L.L. Bean polo shirt and brand new white sneakers.

I quickly assessed the situation and asked, "Is there any reason that your white shirt and shoes would need to remain white?"

"What do you mean?" he said.

Rummaging through the closet I found an old flannel shirt and a pair of rubber boots and handed them to him. Not wanting to call attention to his obvious ranch fashion faux pas, I said, "I think you would be happier dressed like the rest of us."

He surveyed the motley looking crew, consisting of my mom, my husband and myself, standing before him wearing yellow-stained baggy jeans and overalls, flannel shirts, and rubber boots caked with last year's cow poop, topped off with equally blemished Bud Light baseball hats.

I'm sure at that point he must have concluded that it had been a tough year for us financially, as he graciously conceded without another comment, and put on the attire I handed him.

"One more thing," I said as we walked out the door. I handed Tom a pair of gloves, "You'll need these."

"Nah, that's O.K.," he said. "I don't need any gloves."

"Suit yourself," I said and stuffed them in my pocket.

We got the cows and calves sorted without too much effort — that is after the mandatory time it takes to allow a newcomer to play "Rawhide" when they first get a whip into their hands.

My husband lined us out on our duties, my mom and brother would help him at the calf table closing the head and tail gates, administering shots, and etc., while I pushed the calves up the chute.

It took a couple of calves to get any kind of a routine down. I pushed the first calf up to the table and told my brother to open the tailgate so I could let it in. He looked around for a minute and finally said, "Where's the button?"

Once he got over the surprise that there was no button and he had to manually grab the gate and pull it open, he quickly got the hang of it. The first few calves went through pretty smooth and I could see my brother was starting to enjoy himself…that is until the fourth calf. The fourth calf was bigger than most, was stubborn and had a bad case of diarrhea to boot. I got the calf up to the table, but he wouldn't go any further. The more I pushed on him the more he locked his front legs and the more his rear end went up in the air along with the afore mentioned diarrhea.

So my husband said, "Tom, grab that calf by the tail and give it a little twist while Deb pushes on him to get him to move."

Did I mention this calf had really bad diarrhea? Tom took one look at the calf's tail and looked at me in complete disgust.

"That would be the reason for the gloves," I said, as I pulled them out of my pocket and handed them to him. He put on the gloves and gingerly grabbed the calf's tail between his thumb and forefinger, and while holding his breath gave it a gentle twist. About that time I raised myself up on the sides of the chute and shoved him the rest of the way with my feet.

After a few more calves he got the hang of it and was grabbing and twisting tails and wrangling calves like he had been doing it forever. He finally realized, like the rest of us, that calf poop was just part of the job and something you had to put up with. He even quit wrinkling up his nose every time one with diarrhea came through. He did find out the hard way though that you have to be mindful of taking your gloves off before you scratch your nose.

When he helped me push cows through the chute he also quickly learned the reason for the rubber boots, and stopped his futile attempts of trying to step around the cow pies and learned to slide through them like the rest of us.

Being the good sport that he is, it wasn't until the end of the day that we realized the boots we had given him to wear were about a size too small. We all thought he was really getting into the whole ranching thing and was walking like a bow-legged cowboy on purpose — until he took off his boots and had to manually flatten out his curled toes.

I asked him later what he thought about the whole ranching thing and he said it's just like any other business, "The more money you make the more 'crap' you have to put up with."

Now that he's a "seasoned" rancher, next year he says he's bringing his city slicker wife, Belinda. I heard him call her on the phone, "Nah, you'll love visiting here next spring. Just make sure you bring those fancy new leather Italian shoes, you know the ones with the open toes that you paid $200 for, you'll have some good opportunities here to wear them...Yeah, and don't let me forget to throw in my hip waders."

32

Who's The Sheep Dip Here?

AFTER I GOT over my milk cow and chicken phases, I decided sheep would be my next adventure. I thought if Mary could have a little lamb that followed her, by golly so could I. I soon found out that although lambs may be willing to follow you around, ewes don't seem to want you around – this is evidenced by their eagerness to shove you out of the way. Whoever decided that sheep were so docile and serene that they could be used to induce sleep apparently hasn't ever been head butted in the hip by one.

We purchased 16 ewes and I had visions of getting to know each one of them so well that I could tell them apart and give them individual names like "Sweet Pea" and "Honey." Turns out I named them collectively as a flock — "Sheep Dips," a term, which was usually preceded by a few expletives.

The first time I went out in the field to gather the ewes and take them to a new pasture I took my sheepherder's staff. I didn't know at the time why I needed a staff, but I'd seen pictures of sheepherders and they all seemed to have one.

This is when I discovered that they really don't follow you. I could have stood out there until their wool grew so long it hit the ground and they still wouldn't have made any effort to come in my direction. So I figured they must be like cattle, I'll just herd them through the gate. The sheep quickly gathered in a tight little group and proceeded to run almost as one. I thought, wow, this will be a lot easier than cattle; there are no stragglers to go back for.

The only problem was that tight little mass of wool and beady eyes wouldn't run in the direction I wanted them to. As it so happens the field they were in had a road going through it, which acted as a turn around for equipment making a loop around the field. They got on this road and ran around it like runners at a track and field event. Every time I would get in front of them and try to push them back the other way toward the gate, they would just run around the track in the opposite direction.

After two hours I finally figured out what that staff was for. I caught a couple of the ewes around the hind foot with the crooked end and wrestled them through the gate thinking the others might follow if they see one in the other field. But they would squirt back out between my legs before I could get the gate closed and rejoin the other sheep still running the 1/4- mile.

I finally sat down exhausted and realized that the sheep might not be the only dips in the field because I had continued to run around the track after them for the better part of the morning before finally going to get help. With my husband's assistance, we were finally able to herd the sheep through the gate, but even with both of us it wasn't easy.

Shortly after this incident we decided what we really needed was a good sheep-herding dog. So, for 16 ewes, that get moved about once every three weeks, we went out and bought a $1,500 dog. Again, the question of the rightful owner of the title "Sheep Dips" comes to mind...

Don't get me wrong, the dog performed beautifully. After I learned a few of the commands she went out and moved the sheep through the same gate that took me half a day to get them through, in 15 minutes. But, with only that to do once every few weeks, she became bored and took it upon herself to move them whenever she felt like it. Only problem is she couldn't figure out how to open the gate and ended up much like me, running them in circles around the track.

I finally got to where we went out and moved the sheep somewhere every day, just so she would have something to do. But she was a hard worker and that still wasn't enough. She eventually decided to start herding the cattle, horses, pigs, chickens and barn cats by herself. When we really realized we were in trouble though is when she started trying to herd our friends and relatives out to their cars. Unfortunately, our attempts at getting her to herd salesmen away from the house were unsuccessful — if she would have done that we might have kept her around a little longer. But we realized she needed to be on a ranch with more than 16 ewes or we would have to keep her in a kennel, which seemed unfair because all she wanted to do was work, so we sold her.

I did, however, manage to keep the sheep until they lambed that first year. I really didn't know anything about sheep and was so surprised one evening when the first ewe to lamb had twins. I came running back to the house jumping up and down, "We've got twins, we've got twins!"

About an hour later I came running back into the house announcing to anyone who would listen, "We've got triplets! Can you believe it? There are three of the little boogers!"

A few days into lambing and after several more times of me running around excitedly announcing the news of multiple births, someone finally told me that almost all ewes have twins and triplets.

An experienced sheep rancher also told me that if I wanted the sheep to follow me around, all I had to do was grain them. Sure enough, as soon as they figured out what I had in the bucket, every day they ran up to greet me at the feed trough. It even got to where I could pet and scratch them while they ate, although it was more like I was an annoying fly on their backside that they couldn't reach They tolerated me. But like little Mary in the nursery rhyme, everywhere I went the sheep finally did follow me.

All of this makes me wonder though…did Mary's little lamb really follow her to school one day or did she bribe it with a bucket of grain?

33

Ranchers Are All About Style

I HAVE BEEN keeping an eye on the fashion trends these days and I've concluded that ranchers are inherently some of the trendiest dressers around, particularly when it comes to jeans.

Fashion conscious individuals are paying big bucks to get jeans that are what they call "distressed." I'm sure they must have machines that do this sort of thing in the fashion industry that rip them in strategic places, pull threads up from the material and make permanent creases. But ranchers have all of these benefits without paying the extra cost.

The thing is, almost all rancher's jeans are distressed – climb over a couple of barbed wire fences, hook them on a few exposed nails and for permanent creases sit in a tractor seat for three days straight and you've got authentic "distressed" jeans.

Many other jean styles were actually developed by ranchers.

"Wide leg" jeans were invented when cow dogs continually grabbed a hold of a rancher's pant legs and tugged on them while they were walking to the barn. This also contributed to the "distressed" and "frayed' looks and was the precursor to "cutoff" shorts.

"Elastic waist" jeans were made out of necessity as the rancher became more and more fond of pork, and it became impolite to undo your top button and fly at the dinner table.

The popular "push up" jeans, which lift your derriere, have been around for quite some time and began when ranchers started using baling twine to hike up their jeans.

"Boot cut" was developed by ranchers who liked to put on their boots and spurs before their jeans. With the invention of these jeans ranchers felt they had a justification for sleeping with their boots on to speed up the dressing process in the morning, but this style never went over well with rancher's wives.

One of the most popular current styles, "baggy" jeans, were initially invented by ranchers with large families, who being cost conscious, passed jeans down from the older children to the younger as they outgrew them. Unlike city folks though, tripping over the bottoms got in the way of chasing cattle and having the crotches hang down to their knees became a problem when wearing hip high irrigation boots. So instead, they reversed the order and began "handing up" jeans from the younger to the older children and invented the "hipster" and "tight leg" jeans as well as "stretch" jeans.

"Straight leg" jeans were actually the result of ranchers wearing their jeans for three weeks straight without washing them and they discovered their jeans would no longer bend at the knees. It was kind of fun at first, but as with the "baggy" style, there were problems. Cows were not easily intimidated by the comic look of a family of ranchers chasing them with inflexible knees, and laughing cows are not easily herded. Horses were also not fond of this style as ranchers had to be hoisted above the horse by a pulley system to get seated in the saddle.

However, there are some styles of jeans that ranchers only wear when doing specific jobs. The popular "low rise" jeans are only worn while working on the plumbing or doing odd jobs around the house that require a lot of squatting and bending over.

Manufacturers claim that jeans come in several different colors, but upon close observation, it appears they are just in different stages of wearing out. For instance "dark denim" jeans are jeans that have only been washed once or twice. "Medium light" jeans have been washed and worn about 30 times and "light denim" jeans have definitely seen better days.

Ranchers however, were the first to invent the "White wash" color, which are actually jeans that have been worn while cleaning out the chicken coop. And for the "Antique" or "Vintage" color, cow poop provides a nice yellowish worn look to jeans that stays in the material even after numerous washings.

"Bleached" jeans are a spin off from the "Antique" styles that originated with rancher's wives when they tried to get the cow poop out, and "stonewash" jeans are pretty much out of vogue since the invention of the washing machine.

Ranchers have come up with a few styles and colors that haven't reached the fashion industry yet – "grass stained" jeans, "dog slobber" jeans, "pig slop" jeans, "broken fly" jeans, "busted bottom" jeans, "grease tint" jeans, and jeans with various outdoor odors — "scratch and sniff" jeans.

I suspect it's only a matter of time before the rest of the population catches on to these styles as they have the others. It's just a shame that ranchers don't receive any monetary compensation for their worthwhile contributions to the fashion industry.

34

Hot Hay Tarps And Puddin' Head Follies

AUGUST IS A great time of year for ranchers — the water wars are dying down as the rivers drop, calving season is over, feeding hasn't begun and most of the hay is baled and stacked. About the only thing left is the yearly job of covering the haystacks to prevent damage from the rain.

Now, one would think that putting tarps on a haystack wouldn't be too complicated, especially on a stack of baled hay that forms a nice flat surface on top. But, one has never encountered a Puddin' Head.

Puddin' Head is our part black lab, and Lord only knows what, dog. And as her name implies, although quite lovable, she's not Lassie material. To put it mildly, if Timmy were to fall down a well on our ranch, she wouldn't go for help, she wouldn't grab a rope, and she wouldn't even bark to attract attention — she would look down the well wagging her tail and slobber all over the poor little fellow. Fortunately for Timmy, he doesn't come around often.

Puddin' Head does have her good points though. She's friendly, she can run fast, she's friendly, she can jump high and... did I already mention that she's friendly? But let's just say helping cover haystacks isn't one of her stronger attributes, although you do have to give her credit for trying.

It didn't help matters either that we picked the hottest day of the year to stand up on top of a haystack, 25 feet closer to the blazing sun, wrestling with 200 pounds of hot plastic tarp. My husband, Mike, and I, used the conventional ladder method to get to the top of the stack. Puddin' Head on the other hand, got a run at it, jumped and hit the stack about center and managed to claw the rest of the way to the top deftly hooking her toes on baling twine like an experienced mountain climber.

We hadn't expected Puddin' Head to offer to help, but once she was on top of the stack we couldn't see any safe way to get her down so decided to let her stay.

Mike had already placed the rolled up tarps on top of the hay stack with the tractor's grappling hook so all we needed to do was unroll them, easy right? Not with a Puddin' Head. She thought it was a game and began jumping on the tarp as we were unrolling it and tried to help by pulling it with her teeth. This wouldn't have been quite so bad if it weren't for the fact that holes in a tarp kind of defeat its intended purpose.

After thoroughly getting yelled at by both of us, she finally decided not to help quite so much and we managed to get the tarp unrolled. Unfortunately, the tarp ended up lopsided, hanging longer on one side than the other, and wasn't covering the end of the stack.

So Mike decided he would climb down and start fastening the tie downs to see if he could straighten it out and that I should stay on top of the hotter than a pizza oven hay stack in case he needed me to do anything. That's when the real fun began.

I waited for Mike's instructions as he unbeknownst to me began pulling on the tarp from the ground. After about five minutes he yelled up and said, "It must be hung up somewhere, it's not budging. Can you see the problem?"

As I said, I didn't even know he was pulling on it and was still waiting for orders.

"You think it might help if I get off the tarp?" I yelled down to him half laughing.

"Hey, there's an idea," he said. "Why don't you try it...NOW!"

So Puddin' Head and I made our way over to the two-foot wide strip of uncovered hay at one end where the tarp wouldn't reach, and once again began the waiting process in the sweltering heat. We could see bits of tarp tightening around the stack as Mike continued to struggle with it from the ground.

Exasperated, he finally yelled up and said, "It's not working, you are going to have to pull the tarp over the end and down on one side from up there."

If you have never had the privilege of trying to move a hay tarp while incidentally it is also the only place to stand on, it's similar to trying to make the bed while you're still in it. Now image that...and throw a Puddin' Head on top of it to counteract your every move.

Every piece of tarp I grabbed a hold of to pull, Puddin' Head would firmly plant her seat on top of it. A tarp is heavy enough without a dog sitting on it. Add the 101-degree temperature, the uncomfortable feeling of hot plastic against your skin, a man standing at the bottom of the stack yelling orders, and you've got the makings of one cranky rancher's wife.

So it was time to take charge, well, at least whine a little. "Can I get down now?" I yelled.

"Unless I'm suffering from heat stroke and it looks a whole lot different up there than it does down here, NO," he said. "We need to get this done."

So once again I began pulling on the tarp, this time on my hands and knees to get more leverage. I had finally managed to convince Puddin' Head that she couldn't sit on the section of tarp I was pulling on, so she dutifully sat next to me. The only problem with this was that now I was down on all fours at her level, she decided that I needed a good face licking while my hands were busy. Every time I let go of the tarp she would quit, every time I grabbed the tarp she would commence to licking.

I finally had to walk her over to the previously mentioned two-foot wide strip of uncovered hay at the other end of the stack and make her sit. After another good 20 minutes of tugging and sweating I finally managed to pull the hay tarp over the end and evened it out the sides.

"Now can I get down?" I whined again.

"O.K.," he said. "Make sure Puddin' Head comes with you so I can get everything tightened down on the sides."

Puddin' Head? I looked around; she wasn't on the strip of hay. I scanned the tarp; she was nowhere to be seen. Just as I was thinking that she must have decided to get down when no one was looking, I saw a bulge in the tarp. Puddin' had gotten underneath the tarp and had crawled to the middle of the stack under it.

I lifted up the end of the tarp and called to her. She didn't budge. I began to get worried that maybe she got under the tarp and got so hot she passed out or something so I went to the lifeless lump in the center of the stack and gently prodded her. She responded by trying to playfully bite my fingers through the tarp.

So I poked her again, the same response, but this time she moved a little. I had to poke her all the way to the end of the stack slowly edging her out like toothpaste from a tube until she finally popped her head out from under the tarp and was once again standing on the narrow uncovered strip of hay.

Relieved to find out she was O.K. I finally responded to the insistent voice coming from the ground that had been yelling up at us every few minutes, with "Would you two quit playing around and get down here!"

I climbed down the ladder and before I hit the ground, Puddin' Head was at my feet wagging her tail and jumping and biting at my shoes to make me hurry faster. I have no idea how she got down, but I'm beginning to think besides her obvious lineage of black lab, greyhound, cheetah and border collie that she must have a little monkey in her as well.

35

We'll Always Have Our Moose

MOST MORNINGS IN a rancher's life are pretty predictable — the sun comes up with nature's alarm of squalling cats and fighting dogs, and the escaped-cow-induced heartburn is easily quenched with a 1/2 bottle of Extra Strength Mylanta. But Sunday morning was a little different…

As I was getting out of bed, I happened to glance out the window and saw the whole herd of cows and their calves running full bore toward the back pasture. As I stood there in my usual too early in the morning to function, with only half a brain engaged stupor, watching and trying to figure out what the cows were up to, they came to a screeching halt. Fortunately the whole herd had the same idea otherwise there would have been a bovine pile up of hooves over heads and tails over T-bones.

Just when their outstretched front legs almost brought them to a stop, they simultaneously whirled around and commenced their charge like a band of liquored up Vikings in the direction they had just come from.

I finally woke up enough to yell down the stairs to my husband, Mike, who was sipping his morning cup of slap-me-in-the-face and wake me up coffee.

"What's wrong with your cows?"

"Same thing that's always wrong with your cows — they're spoiled," he said. It's funny how when there is a problem with the cows, ownership dramatically changes, had they been acting any stranger we probably would have disowned them altogether and said, "What's wrong with the neighbor's cows?"

Still upstairs, I could hear Mike shuffle around the kitchen making his way to the window while muttering something about, dumb cows, cold coffee and no breakfast in sight.

The cows were still continuing their early morning pasture charges running back and forth, only now they had tired to the point that they couldn't run in a straight line and were zigzagging all over the field barely able to miss colliding with each other.

Mike finally got a handle on the situation, "There's a big black mule in the pasture," he exclaimed.

"Where in the world would a mule come from?" I asked. "I don't recall seeing mules at any of the neighbors."

In order to get a better handle on the situation we decided to get a closer view and this started a 10-minute frenzy of ransacking the house for the binoculars. Now ordinarily, the binoculars are sitting on the kitchen table in the way, laying on the couch for some poor unsuspecting soul to plop down on or on the desk anchoring down a stack of unpaid bills. But of course, on this morning when we actually needed them, they were nowhere to be found.

Finally, I found them hanging on a hook that we had specifically placed on the wall several years ago to hang them on.

"How in the world did they get there?" I asked.

"I don't know," said Mike a little exasperated. "We need to quit making designated places to put things, it messes us up."

Fortunately, the "black mule" was still standing there watching the cattle frenzy. Mike took one look through the binoculars and said, "It's a moose!"

"Yeah right," I quipped. "Did you put a little something extra in your coffee this morning? We don't have moose in eastern Oregon, I'm sure it's an elk."

"See for yourself," his said.

So I peered through the binoculars, still strapped around his neck and said, "Whoa, it is a moose!"

After five minutes of jerking the binoculars back and forth until Mike complained of binocular strap burn around his neck, a common ailment with married ranchers, we watched as the moose, growing tired of the cows, stretched out his long legs and nonchalantly stepped over the fence.

The cows of course stood in amazement as they watched the moose trot off into the hills. They didn't say so, but I'm sure they were in awe of an animal that didn't have to squirt through the barbed wires scratching his back, run for a gate inadvertently left open or make a group tackle on a fence post to escape. I've noticed the last few days the cows have been doing more leg stretching exercises.

Mike and I decided to jump in the pickup and see if we could track this long-legged gangly critter down to prove his existence. Stories like this are much more plausible if you have a picture.

Of course we took our trusty hunting dog, Puddin' Head. She's not very good at duck hunting, and she can't heel a cow, so we figured maybe she's a moose dog. As we drove around through the back hills and repeatedly asked her, "Where's the moose? Find "Bullwinkle," we soon discovered she is more interested in Bullwinkle's sidekick "Rocky." Every squirrel she saw, she bounded around in the cab of the pickup slobbering and clawing up our arms and legs in her excitement.

We never did see Bullwinkle again, but several others in our area have reported moose sightings, making it possible to tell our story without suffering the backlash of unbelievers. I know it's a small thing, but since we don't live close enough to Mount St. Helens to watch it erupt, and hurricane Ivan completely missed us, we will always have our moose to talk about.

36

Caution, Slippery When Wet

IT WAS A dark and stormy night, but then it's always a dark and stormy night when cows are having trouble calving. Heaven forbid they should give birth to a breech calf or a 150-pound mammoth baby on a nice sunny afternoon!

A cow could be straining for an hour, and when you go out to check her in good weather, she will stop and walk away nonchalantly whistling as if everything is O.K. And if she knows she is going to have problems, she will actually cross her legs and hold that calf in until nightfall, and then only try to have it if she senses a blizzard approaching.

So, as I was saying, it was a dark and stormy night around 9 p.m. The wind was blowing hard and the skies had chosen this night to dump a month's worth of rain all at once. In the middle of this outburst of Mother Nature, my husband, Mike, and I went out to check a cow that an hour before had looked like she was getting ready to calve.

As soon as the cows heard the four-wheeler coming, they scattered, similar to the balls on a pool table after a break, into all four corners. Only, unlike the pool balls, the cows kept shuffling around exchanging positions making it hard with a spotlight to tell which ones we had already looked at. I'm convinced they do this on purpose because I can always hear them snickering amongst themselves on these occasions.

Once we found the cow that's trying to have a baby, there was, as always, a little group of interested cows hovering around her watching. To see what's going on we had to go in and break it up like detectives on a crime scene, "Nothing here to see girls, move along now, go on back to your corners and graze."

So once we got past all of their usual shenanigans, this particular cow had just given birth and was standing about 25 feet from her newborn calf watching as it struggled to get up. Thank goodness, I thought, it looks O.K., now we can go back to the house and get warm. But, as we examined the situation a little closer, something looked amiss. The calf looked like it was doing fine, but the mother hadn't bothered to lick it off as is the custom among cows.

While we were sitting on the four-wheeler in the drenching rain pondering this situation, all of the sudden the cow let out a huge bellow and stampeded toward her calf at a dead run and stopped about 12 inches short of trampling it. She then proceeded to butt it around with her head.

Now, I'm no expert, but I think this cow had been contemplating what had just happened to her, and after assessing the situation she had finally figured out the source of all her pain and was more than slightly annoyed at it. Having witnessed this type of mad cow behavior before, during their postnatal phase, we sat and watched for a few more minutes to see if she would settle down and start taking care of it.

But, seeing us huddled on the four-wheeler shivering in the shadows, I'm sure the cow decided that since she had no problems having the calf, she would take advantage of this situation anyway, like most cows would, to keep us out in the nasty weather longer. So she proceeded to get really aggressive with the calf and acted like she was going to grind it into the mud with her head.

My husband was driving so he said, "Quick, chase her away from the calf." So I jumped off the four-wheeler and ran up to her just in time to see the glare of her eyes shimmering through the rain before she turned and started running after me.

So I made a hasty retreat to the only nearby protection — the other side of the four-wheeler where Mike was still sitting. After tiring of watching the circus of me running circles around him with the cow in hot pursuit, Mike finally stepped off the four-wheeler between me and the cow, and in a very calm, but demanding tone said, "Git out of here you old bitty."

There was a brief moment of indecision as the cow and I both stopped and looked at each other wondering which one of us he was referring to. I finally said, "I think he means you sister, so scoot!" She reluctantly turned and shuffled off to join the cow congregation that had now gathered to watch the evening's events.

"What in the heck were you doing?" Mike said.

"Well wasn't it obvious?" I said. "I was using myself as a decoy to lure her away from her calf!"

Not wanting to witness another raging female that night, he offered encouragingly, "Well, I guess it kind of worked."

With the cow out of the way, we quickly turned our attention to the calf that was still flaying around on the ground trying to stand up.

"We'll have to get the calf into the barn and then go get the cow and bring her in and milk her and see if we can get this little guy fed," Mike said.

He instructed me to get on the back of the four-wheeler — of course that's where ranch wives always ride when the dog isn't along — and he maneuvered the slimy, wet calf onto the rack behind me. I grabbed one of his legs on each side of me and wrapped him around my waist like a rather large fanny pack as Mike steered us to the barn.

The barn is on the other side of the corrals so Mike dropped the calf and I off in front of the corral gate and said, "Get him into the barn and I'll go get the cow."

No problem…or so I thought. I leaned over to pick up the 80-pound calf by wrapping my arms around his chest and he immediately proceeded to squirt out of my hands. He was so slimy and slippery from the birth and the rain that I couldn't hang on to him. So I tried picking him up by hanging on a little lower around his middle, and the same thing happened — he slid right down to the ground. I even tried picking him up upside down by his rump first, and that didn't do either one of us any favors, in fact, when he slid down this time I went with him. Every time I just about got him picked up and would take a step or two toward the barn he would shoot out of my hands like a big fish.

After about 10 minutes of this, I was covered in slime and mud, and was wet from head to toe, and had only made about 20 feet of progress in my quest for the barn.

I finally had to stop and rest, and while I was waiting to catch my breath, Mike who was nearing the corrals with the cow yelled and said, "You did know that he could probably walk by now didn't you?"

"Errrr, yeah…sure, I was just getting ready to let him do that," I said as I turned and lifted the calf to a standing position.

"O.K. little guy," I said to the calf, "let's get you in the barn." He just stood there. I nudged him with my knees; he still just stood there. I pushed and lifted on his rump, which immediately went up into the air while he braced his front legs in the locked position.

"Alright, if that's the way you want it," I told the calf, "I'll use your hind legs and steer you like a wheelbarrow." I soon found out that trying to pick up a slimy calf's hind legs and hold onto them when he was now old enough to offer some resistance, isn't much easier than trying to pick up the whole slimy calf.

After several attempts, I finally threw up my arms in disgust and said, "That's it, I give up. You can just stay out here." I turned and started to walk toward the barn thinking that I would at least open the doors for Mike to get the cow in, when I went about 10 steps and heard this faint little moo. I looked over my shoulder and the calf was following me.

"Nah," I told myself, "it couldn't be this easy." So I took a few more steps and the calf came running up behind me again. "We'll I'll be darned," I said, "it looks like you finally decided to cooperate." In the process, he had apparently also decided out of desperation that I was his only hope at getting some food and he started butting me. Fortunately he wasn't old enough to do much damage, and he eventually butted me all the way into the barn.

About that time, the cow, with Mike following, came bursting into the barn. I was standing in a corner of the barn and had nowhere to go to get out of her way, so I clenched my body preparing for the worst and waited for her to take her frustration out on me. She came right up to me and sniffed my coat, which was covered in calf slime, and began licking me. Feeling a little uncomfortable with this sudden show of affection, especially after our earlier encounter, I shoved the calf that had been standing behind me in front of her nose and she started licking him instead, apparently she was no longer mad at the little guy.

"Just wait till he becomes a teenager," I told her, "and you'll be mad all over again."

37

The Handyman vs. The Handyma'am

I'VE ALWAYS CONSIDERED myself pretty handy around the house as far as taking care of minor plumbing problems, vacuum cleaner repairs and putting up shelves. Not so much because I really enjoy this type of work, but because I've learned over the years that if you ask a man to do it, you are looking at a minimum of three weeks before you see any results.

For instance, if you ask your husband to hang a painting on the wall you should allow for, at the very least, four straight days of nagging him to do it. Then, it will take a good week of him complaining about your nagging and reiterating how he never has any time to just sit and relax (mainly because he is spending all of his time complaining about your nagging). After that's settled it takes at least another week for the guilt to set in and maybe even a call from his mother before any action is taken.

When the big day finally arrives the tool belt comes out with several different gadgets attached because no job around the house can be performed by a man without a minimum of five tools, and it usually takes more. And keep in mind, this is not a good time to say, "For crying out loud all I want is a nail in the wall" or you may never get that painting out of the closet and into view.

The first thing he always asks you is where you want the painting. Having had three weeks to mull this over you have a pretty good idea and tell him exactly where you would like to see it. But you probably won't get it there because he wouldn't want to put a 1/2-inch nail into a weight-bearing wall for fear of compromising the integrity of the entire house. Besides, it might interfere with his ability to recline the Lay-Z-Boy should he ever decide to move it to that wall. Or later you may find that the real reason is because that is the exact spot he had planned on hanging that impressive life-size fuzzy velvet portrait of five dogs of various breeds sitting at a table playing poker.

Once the "correct" place is finally selected for the painting, the stud finder comes out of the tool belt. After 10 minutes of him placing the stud finder on himself and saying, "Oh look, it found me!" he finally puts it on the wall only to discover your house was built without the use of studs. This is a real turning point in the project and careful planning on the wife's part will determine whether or not he will continue with it. Upon further inspection the wife finds that he drained the batteries playing with the stud finder and pulls out spare batteries from her emergency stash.

Once it is determined that there is indeed a stud in the room, other than the one hanging the painting, out comes the measuring tape. There are few things that men like to do more than measuring. In fact while trying to talk your husband into doing a job like this, it's a good idea to get out his tape measure and entice him with it before hand.

First the painting is measured on all sides to determine if the creator of the frame was off one-thousandth of an inch, which could throw the entire project out of whack. Then the room is measured from floor to ceiling and from end to end to find the exact center of the wall, Unfortunately, that doesn't coincide with any of the studs he found so he decides to measure himself and see how tall he is now. This leads to a trip to the bathroom to weigh himself and then to the kitchen for that leftover lasagna.

Again, the prudent wife will get out the measuring tape, which no man can resist, and entice him back to the job. Once the perfect spot is calculated he places a small dot on the wall with a pencil. At this point the wife would be really tempted to say "Don't you need to mark it a little larger so you can find it again?" but please refrain, this could shut down the entire project. Once he comes back from getting his cordless drill and discovers this for himself, he will undoubtedly say that he needs to recalculate the "perfect spot" again to make sure his figures are correct.

The pull of the tape measure is just too strong and he may

go through the measuring process several times before actually performing the work. If he starts coming toward you with the measuring tape, this is the perfect time to get him that piece of banana cream pie you have been saving and offer it to him.

After the lengthy drill bit selection, which has to be the perfect size for the perfect nail, which took considerable time to choose from his four tier nail bin, he is finally ready to make a hole in the wall. This has to be done with great care as the drill hole has to be perfectly straight and not tilted to one side or the other even a fraction of an inch or the husband will have to exhibit his putting skills. So this is a good time to hold your breath and hope for the best.

Once the hole is drilled to his satisfaction, the nail is hammered in with a special dual head non-rebounding hammer. After inspecting his work he goes back to the kitchen for the rest of the lasagna.

This is another crucial point in the project. If you want to see your painting make it to the wall do everything you can to prevent him from turning the T.V. on to the sports channel. Even though he will tell you he can watch it and do the work at the same time don't fall for this ploy. Put on a negligee, perform the rumba, and get out the Karaoke machine if you have to, but don't let him touch the T.V.

Once he places the painting on the nail, then he needs to get out the level. Leveling the painting could take some time. Not because it's difficult, but because men become fascinated with watching that little bubble to see if they can move the level across the entire top of the painting without it moving. In fact, if video game manufacturers could come up with a game that requires the player to put the bubble in the center every man in America would own one.

You may think at this point the job is done, but then comes the two days of bragging about his work where you show your family, friends, neighbors — even the dog — what a good job he did. Because at some point you may want him to do something else around the house.

So as you can see asking a man to hang a painting is a very

long-term project and the reason why a lot of women become handy around the house. If a woman were to hang a painting she would select a wall, grab a nail out of a rusty coffee can, pound it in the wall with a rock, shoe, T.V. remote or whatever is available and hang the picture by eyeballing it.

But one word of caution, if you decide to be the do-it-yourself wife, don't ever let him see you using a table knife as a screwdriver; I've noticed this can send them into a frenzy.

38

Yucking It Up On The Ranch

AFTER A FIFTY-hour week at work I came home last Friday night about 8 p.m. exhausted. Following a quick dinner I went to bed with instructions to my husband, Mike, not to wake me until noon Saturday, and only then if the house was burning down and for some reason he couldn't pack the bed out with me in it.

So I was less than shall we say "polite" when at 9:30 p.m. I was awakened by a familiar sound.

"Deeeeeear.....I have something for you," he yelled from downstairs.

"What?" I snapped, "for your sake I hope the house is fully engulfed!"

"It's a surprise, come look," he continued.

I managed to crawl out of bed and look over the stair railing and there he stood with a wet black bundle under each arm dripping into slime puddles on the floor.

"It's twins!" he exclaimed.

The only way to describe a calf in those first moments when it comes out of a cow is "yucky." They appear to have the makings of a 24-egg omelet smeared into their hairy little hides. In most cases their moms can look past the goo and give them a proper cleaning, however I have seen more than a few take one look and run the other way. I tried that the first couple of times I was asked to be a surrogate mother to one of these slimy little creatures, but like the cows, my husband tracked me down and made me come back.

"Alright," I conceded, "get them into the bathroom."

It was a really cold and stormy evening and the calves being so small and weak were too cold to stand so the first priority was to get them dried off and warm.

I threw a tarp on the floor that we keep handy for just such an emergency and Mike one by one let them slide out of arms onto it. With a small floor heater, two blow driers and an electric heating pad going the room very quickly became a 105-degree calf incubator.

Keep in mind that our bathroom is pretty small and take into account with the enamel fixtures and shower, there is only about six feet of floor space left. The sprawled out calves took up about four and half feet of the space so as we worked on warming the calves and drying them with towels and the afore mentioned blow driers, Mike and I maneuvered over the last foot and a half of floor space straddling the calves like playing a game of Twister. Right foot to white-faced calf's left ear, left hand to green toilet seat (lid closed of course)…And then there was the occasional, "eeeew, I just got my hand in something gooey — make way – I've got to get to the sink."

When calves are this cold and wet it takes considerable time and lots of towels to dry them off before they show signs of life. Finally, after more than two hours of drying, the calves were sitting upright, and as the clock in the next room chimed midnight, our patience and our backs were on their last legs.

We wrestled around for another half hour getting some milk, which Mike had extracted from the not so willing cow earlier, down them and decided they were in good shape for the night.

As we stood and surveyed the slime-strewn room, I silently pointed to the pile of yucky, soaked towels on the floor.

"What?" he said.

"Can you please pick them up?" I asked.

"Why can't you pick them up?" he said.

"You're closer to them," I replied.

He stepped back a few inches, "Not any more!"

Which in turn, I stepped back two inches. "Oh yes, I think you are," I said.

We kept stepping back a few inches at a time until we had climbed over the calves and were at opposite ends of the bathroom against the walls, which isn't very far apart in such a small room. We glared at each other like two gunfighters in a cheap western movie, both waiting for the other to "reach for it" and pick up the towels.

My arm twitched and I leaned forward slightly, and immediately retracted when I saw the smile of satisfaction spread across his face. After a few more minutes he sighed and shifted his weight to bend over. I thought I have him now he's going in for the towels. No such luck, he merely bent over to scratch his leg.

Finally, the standoff ended when one of the calves struggled into a standing position and bawled.

"Oh look," I exclaimed, "they're going to be O.K."

At that point I would like to say that also, similar to the movies, our eyes met, our souls touched, and we walked out of the bathroom smiling hand in hand, but at 1 a.m. who has the energy for such nonsense? Instead we continued to battle over who was going to pick up the towels for another 10 minutes until we decided to each pick up half and then went our separate ways to get cleaned up and ready for bed.

We fell into bed grumbling and complaining about sore knees, strained backs and lack of sleep, only to wake up two hours later to check the heifers. But you know, I wouldn't trade this lifestyle for anything because contrary to the way calves look when they are first born, once dried off and de-slimed, they are about the cutest little critters God ever created. I just need to keep reminding myself of that every time I step into or put my hand into something yucky.

39

The Bleeping Beep Beep

AFTER A FULL day of mending fences, my muscles were sore, my hands were blistered and I was dog-tired. Not the kind of tired like a snoozing dog who keeps one ear flap open and an alert snout to sniff the evening breeze for dead rodents, but the Puddin' Head kind of tired.

After Puddin' Head, our black Lab, Chihuahua, St. Bernard and Lord only knows what cross, spends the day chasing the four-wheeler, tractor, grasshoppers or anything else that has the unfortunate side affect of moving, she lies flat on her back. Her legs are sprawled in all directions, her mouth gapes open, and her tongue hits the floor and rolls out like a fly strip waiting for insects to adhere to it. For all practical purposes she's dead to the world. Not a very pretty sight, but I don't care. That's how tired I was – Puddin' Head tired.

As soon as my head hit the pillow, I assumed the position. It would have been a good time for a grizzly bear to pay a visit because I could have won an Oscar for playing dead. Nothing, not an earthquake, aerial attack of killer tomatoes or buckets of ice water to the face would have woke me — if it hadn't been for that blasted beep.

The first couple of beeps I heard, I easily incorporated into to my dream: You want me to pitch how much of that beep beep hay into those beep beep feed bunks for your beep beep cows! (I know it's getting close to winter when I start having feeding dreams.) But, alas, there are only so many beeps you can use in a dream before you realize that they are coming from somewhere beyond your sleep realm.

"What's that beeping?" I asked as I nudged my husband, Mike, in the ribs.

"It's your cell phone," he said groggily, "go shut it off."

So I trudged down the stairs, got my cell phone out of my purse and ended its connection with the world for the night. I just got back upstairs and when my head hit the pillow, we heard it again – beep beep.

"It must be your cell phone," I told Mike. It was then his turn to go downstairs and hit the power off button to his yak box and say "cell ya later" to would be callers.

O.K., now back to the business of sleeping…. beep beep. Can the cell phones make a noise when they are turned off we wondered… Just then Mike said, "I know, it's got to be a dead battery in one of the smoke alarms." He stomped back down the stairs, and pretty soon I heard chairs moving and plastic popping along with a few swear words as he proceeded to disconnect every alarm in the house.

Back in bed again, he said, "There, that should take care of it."

Beep beep….

"That wasn't it," I said.

That prompted a mass search by both of us. We turned off all the digital clocks in the house, and checked the microwave, the oven, the stereo, T.V., computer, VCR, dishwasher, clothes dryer, and even Puddin' Head who of course was still asleep during all of this.

After we were satisfied that we had turned off and unplugged everything electronic in the house, we went back to bed…only to be serenaded by the bleeping beep beep again.

"It almost sounds like it's coming from outside," I said. "I wonder if it's my car?"

Mike flew out of bed and went outside to investigate the new Subaru that I had purchased just a couple of days before. A few minutes later he came back in and reported that there was a light on in my car, which might be making the noise and that I needed to figure out how to turn it off.

So we were both outside circling my car like a couple of sleep-deprived, pajama-clad burglars peeping in the windows trying to figure out what the lit up button said. Every time we opened the car door the light went off and it couldn't be read.

"Maybe if we get in and close the doors, it will light up again," I said.

As we were both sitting in the front seats of my Subaru, we discovered the red light said, "Security."

"Well, turn it off," said Mike, " so we can get some sleep."

"I don't know how to turn it off," I said as I grabbed the owner's manual out of the jockey box.

Just as I found the section that said, "The security indicator light deters potential thieves by indicting that the vehicle is equipped with an immobilizer system" and was reading it out loud, Mike said, "what's this button do?" and pushed it. He set off the car alarm and the horn began honking and the lights began flashing. The security light may deter thieves, but apparently not sleepy ranchers.

I began feverously flipping through the manual trying to find how to turn that commotion off. This is one of those moments where you thank the good Lord that you are a rancher and live out in the country away from neighbors who can't see you sitting in your car at 1 a.m. in your pajamas with the alarm going off.

After about three ear-splitting minutes, I found how to turn it off in the manual, which by the way isn't set up in an easy to read format for the cranky and sleep deprived. I may have to alert Subaru to that issue.

Finally, we got everything turned off, went back into the house, tripped over the dog who was still sprawled out on the floor asleep and crawled back into bed.

"You know, I never did hear the car make that beep beep sound while we were out there, did you? I asked. "Maybe that's not what was making the noise."

Just then somewhere off in the distance, as I was about to doze off, I heard a faint, lone coyote howl. Puddin' Head, who had slept through horns honking, furniture moving, people stomping around cussing and the annoying beep beep, bolted upright, sucked in her tongue, and began howling a response, which in turn got the coyote howling more.

We've learned from past experience that there is nothing we can do to get her to stop this primal exchange with a wild animal until she's darn good and ready, so we waited. In the mean time, we heard another noise... It sounded like the tone you hear when you pick up a telephone.

"What in the heck is that?" asked Mike.

"It sounds like my laptop computer is trying to connect to the Internet," I said. "Hey, I wonder if that's what's been making the beep beep noise all this time too."

Mike jumped out of bed and went tearing down the stairs.

"Where are you going?" I called after him.

"I'm not taking any chances," he said. "I'm going to put your laptop, our cell phones, and the dog in your Subaru and drive them down to the barn for the night."

A few minutes later after he returned, and as we were finally approaching slumber, I had a thought. I jabbed Mike in the ribs, "Hey, what if we have a fire? All of the alarms are disabled."

Mike sat up in bed, turned on the light, looked me directly in the eyes and said, "Do you want to join the dog in the car?"

With the proper incentive, it's amazing how fast sleep can come...

40

Doing The Chute Shovel And Stomp

LIVING IN THE state's Icelandic region, eastern Oregon ranchers are familiar with all kinds of snow removal devices — tractors with blades, snow blowers, four-wheelers with pieces of plywood tied on the front and just letting visitors and the UPS driver get stuck in your driveway a few times removes some of the snow when they try to dig their way out. But the most commonly used rancher's snow removal device is a rancher's wife.

Give her a snow shovel and the right incentive and she can move a lot of snow in a short period of time. Make her mad, and she can move an entire mountain. I know, because I am one of these snow removal devices.

Last weekend my husband placed me into service digging out snow from the corral gates and the loading chute so we could take a few steers to the sale.

The main alleyway in the corrals was buried in about three feet of snow. As he saw me standing there contemplating how in the world I was going to shovel out all of that snow he came up with an idea.

"Why don't you march up and down that alley about 20 times and smash the snow down so the calves won't mind going in there," he said. "I think that will work just as well and you won't have to shovel so much."

Thus I began my job as a combo snow removal-stomper device while he pushed snow around in the areas that were wide enough for the tractor to fit in.

I marched up and down the alley about five times and managed to make a trail that sank into the hard crusty snow about two inches deep before I heard Mike stop the tractor.

"That's not going to work," he yelled from across the corrals. "You've got to stomp harder."

"I am stomping hard," I said as I jumped up and down still bouncing off the top of the snow.

"Harder than that," he said as he came closer.

So I stomped around some more still not making much headway.

'You've got to put your whole body into it," he said. "You're not trying hard enough."

I was getting pretty irritated at this point partly because I wasn't making any progress and mostly because ranch wives, as ranchers will attest, don't particularly like being told what to do. So I mustered up all of my strength, jumped into the air and did a full body slam just like I'd seen them do on Saturday night wrestling and I fell through the top layer of snow all the way to the bottom.

"That's it," he said. "Now just keep doing that all the way down the alley until you have it smashed down."

About an hour and 20 body slams later, I was too tired to go on and didn't have even a 1/4 of the snow smashed down yet. The jumping up and slamming myself down in the snow wasn't the hard part – it was the recovery time in between and crawling back up to a standing position that was wearing me out.

To make the situation worse, our black lab, Puddin' Head thought I was playing and every time I slammed down to the ground she jumped on my head.

As I was lying there flaying around in the snow like a beached whale in my insulated Carhart overalls with a dog chewing on my ears trying to get up, I heard the tractor stop again.

He walked over to me and said, "We're never going to get this done if you keep laying around playing with Puddin'," he said. "I guess I'll just have to do it myself, why don't you go shovel the snow out by the gate next to the barn."

"Great," I said rather sarcastically. "I'd like to see you do it!"

I had envisioned stomping off in a huff, but it's kind of hard when you have to roll around on the ground for five minutes to get to a place where you can even get your feet under you.

By the time I finally did get up though, I showed him. I grabbed the shovel and stomped over to the barn and began flinging snow from the massive heap that had built up over the winter so fast that it made his head spin Actually I thought it had made his head spin, but he was just looking the other way and hadn't even noticed my little outburst. There's nothing worse that wasting a good tirade on someone who's not even paying attention.

I stopped shoveling snow long enough to watch and see how he had decided to handle the situation in the alleyway. He walked over and stomped around on the snow unsuccessfully for a few minutes and headed back toward the tractor.

"Ha," I yelled. "Too much for ya, huh?"

He just kept walking without saying a word and went past the tractor to the hay pile. He grabbed a large flake of hay and came back and scattered it up and down the alleyway where I had spent the better part of the morning stomping.

He then opened a gate, which led into the corral from a nearby pen that held a dozen steers. He stood back as the steers ambled into the alley and I watched while they stomped every last flake of snow down to the ground in about five minutes.

"Well why in the heck didn't you do that before?" I asked.

"You know, I never thought of it," he said. "If I had spread out a big cheesecake in there for you, you probably would have finished the job a lot faster too."

41

We're A Rockin', But We're Not Rollin'

BEING A RANCHER'S wife and living 25 miles out of town, I have had to endure all types of driving conditions — snow, sleet, ice, fog, hail, wind and backseat drivers. (I would have placed wind and backseat drivers in the same category, but I think most vehicles are already equipped with something similar called an air bag.) So having to drive pickups, tractors and four-wheelers in all of these types of conditions has made me pretty confident in my ability to maneuver a vehicle around in less than perfect conditions — including the foot of new snow that we received one night a few weeks ago.

As I was preparing for work the next morning my husband, Mike, asked me if he needed to plow the driveway, which is about 1/4 mile long, before he went out to feed the cattle so my son, Jake, and I could get to town.

"Nah," I said. "I can get through that, I've got four-wheel drive and I've driven through more snow than this. I've even had to walk through more snow than this to get to school as a kid, five feet to be exact…three miles of it in blinding blizzards…one time barefoot…"

"O.K., O.K.," he interrupts. "You can stop, I get your point. I'll go feed the cows and see you tonight."

With that Jake and I hopped in my pickup and headed down the driveway…well…where I thought the drive way should be… It had snowed so much that the slopes along the sides of the driveway had filled in making the road level with the adjacent pasture and I couldn't tell where the road was.

As I was maneuvering my pickup through the snow on the non-visible road, trying to remember exactly how close the road was to the haystack, Jake broke my concentration yelling, "You're going off the road, turn your wheels!" I figured he should know because he has been telling me how to drive ever since he got his driver's license and became an expert, so I cranked the wheels hard to the right.

"No," he yelled. "The other way." So I rotated to the left.

"No," he yelled again. "Straighten them up."

As I zigged and zagged across the road, he continued to shout directions until I came to a halt, which would have been O.K. had I intended to stop, but the pickup just wouldn't go any further. It seems that Jake's "careful" guidance and my apparent inability to follow directions landed us sideways in the irrigation ditch that runs parallel to the drive way.

I didn't have to ponder what had happened more than a split second though because Jake quickly assessed the situation for me.

"Well you're off the road now," he said. "Didn't you hear me tell you to straighten the wheels?"

It's times like this that it's nice to have an expert driver along to tell you exactly what went wrong and it's even better when they tell you what you need to do about it.

"Just go forward and back until you get it to rocking," he said. "Once you get to rocking fast enough, the momentum will squirt you back onto the road."

"I don't know," I said cautiously. "Mike will be done feeding in a few minutes and he can just pull us out with the tractor. He has chains on the tires."

"Heck, I've gotten out of deeper holes than this before, just try it," he said.

Once again heeding the expertise of my insistent passenger, who assured me this technique would propel me out of the two-feet deep ditch, I did as he said.

After about 10 minutes of rockin' and not rollin', I said, "What's that smell? It smells like burning rubber."

Like inspector Holmes trying to solve a mystery, Jake got out and looked the situation over. "Well," he said, "The tires are starting to smoke a little...they're probably cheap ones or they wouldn't have gotten this hot from spinning out...I guess I better go get Dad's diesel truck and a chain," he said as he was walking back toward the house.

Since my side of the pickup was buried in the snow and my door wouldn't open, I decided it was pointless to remind him that Mike would be coming up the driveway with the tractor in a few minutes. But, just as I was pondering this possibility I looked down the hill where Mike was feeding and noticed that all of the calves that had been weaned a few weeks ago had escaped and were running into the pasture where the cows were.

I thought about going back to the house to get my boots and help him out, but about that time Jake had showed up with Mike's truck.

Jake hooked a chain between the trucks and gave me instructions to keep the wheels of my pickup straight, put it in reverse and floorboard it, while he pulled me out. So at the same time we simultaneously pushed the pedal to the metal and Jake shot down the driveway like a rocket cleared for take off. He almost made it back to the house before he noticed that my pickup hadn't budged — it seems the chain had come loose.

"Don't worry," he said as he hooked up the chain again. "That was just a practice run, I wanted to see how much torque I would need to give Mike's truck to get it down the driveway."

The next time we tried the chain held tight, but because of all the previous rocking we had done, it had created some considerable ruts inside the ditch and one of my back wheels wasn't even touching the ground so it still wouldn't budge. But he was persistent.

After about 10 minutes of backing up next to my pickup and getting a run at it, as I was rubbing my neck, which felt like it had sustained whiplash from all of the rocking and jerking, he came running up to my pick up and said, "Well there's the problem, I told you to keep the wheels straight. I would have had you out a long time ago if the wheels had been straight."

"I'm in my truck buried in three feet of snow in a ditch and I can't open the door," I said. "How am I supposed to be able to look and see if the wheels are straight?"

Giving me that I understand because you're a woman look,

which I'm sure he learned from Mike by the way, he guided me as I steered the wheels into a straight position.

And as it turns out he was correct, my pickup started to move! I thought, I just might make it to work after all. Unfortunately, he just dragged me down the ditch about 50 yards. I thought about asking him if the reason we couldn't get back up onto the road had anything to do with the wheels being too straight, but at about that time Mike came down the driveway in the tractor.

After having to chase cows and calves around for the last half hour and then seeing what a mess we had created in the driveway with my pickup buried in the ditch with his truck still hooked to it, I thought he would be pretty irritated. But he just stepped out of the tractor, looked around for a minute said, "Well did you at least remember to wait for the glow plug on my truck, it's a diesel you know?"

Five minutes later he had pulled me out of the ditch with the tractor, and Jake and I were ready to go to town again. As I got into the driver's seat, Jake started giving me instructions again.

He said," This time keep the wheels straight and don't go to the left again...and stay away from the right side.... and when you come to that corner..." but before he could finish, I tossed him the keys and said, "Here, you drive." He did, and he maneuvered the pickup down the driveway and through the snow to the main road effortlessly. And I must say that I have never gone down our driveway that fast before or had my knuckles ever turn that white from hanging on to the dashboard. But as he continued to point out even days later — I could have avoided that entire situation had I let him drive in the first place. Geesh, if I'd only known!

42

Calf Butt Patrol or Oh, Yeah, I Meant to Tell You

CALVING IS FINALLY over, but now the diarrhea season is upon us. Every day we walk through the cows and check their youngsters for signs of coccidiosis, an illness they get from drinking out of contaminated puddles of water. They have fresh running water just steps away from them at all times, but invariably they go out of their way, crossing fences, mountains the size of Everest and swimming rivers with white water rapids to find a dirty puddle to drink out of.

I think the cows put them up to it as part of their ninja kicking training or something. "My son, in order to see the great white calf, you must first drink from the puddle of knowledge, then all good things will come to you, including the runs."

At any rate, early detection and treatment of this disease is crucial so we patrol the herd daily looking at messy rear ends like Sherlock Holmes after his arch nemesis. Once you spot a calf with the afore mentioned posterior condition, you have to determine if it is indeed coccidiosis or just a calf that has imbibed in too much milk. The only sure way to tell is to watch it "in action."

Some people call their spouses and say, "Guess what, honey, I just got a promotion and a raise!" Ranchers call their spouses and say, "Guess what, honey, the calf just pooped and it looks normal!"

Once you do find a calf, however, that has coccidiosis, treatment is very difficult, not because giving it an antibiotic shot and sulfa pills is hard, but because you have to catch it first!

A two-month old calf with coccidiosis may look and act sick, as if it has no energy and is just barely dragging itself around the field, but get hold of it and it will be dragging you around.

Last week there was a calf in the herd that was so miserable it was walking like its rear end was competing with its head for the lead position. My husband, Mike, tiptoed up behind it and grabbed the calf by the back leg with a 10-foot pole with a hook on the end. The calf, that only moments before would have qualified as a poster child for sloth-like behavior, immediately came to life and started running.

I grabbed onto the pole behind Mike in an attempt to help slow it down, but only succeeded in letting it drag both of us around the field. We must have looked like we were playing an old schoolyard game of crack the whip as the calf zigzagged us back and forth across the pasture thrashing me around at the end of a pole.

In all the commotion Mike somehow managed to slip a rope around the calf's foot. With me manning the pole and him the rope we got the calf in a different gear – reverse – and pulled him over to the four-wheeler. Mike instructed me to keep holding onto the calf with the pole while he tried to tie the rope off to the four-wheeler.

While I was still wrestling with the calf on the end of the pole, Mike with his back to me said, "I meant to tell you whatever you do don't get between the calf and the four- wheeler."

"Too late," I croaked as he turned to find me sprawled across the four-wheeler on my back with my legs strapped to it like a damsel in distress on the railroad tracks.

My hero maneuvered the calf back around the four- wheeler to release the rope that bound me, but before I could get upright and off my back the calf, still tied, took off on three legs dragging the four-wheeler.

"Oh yeah, I meant to tell you to put the Honda in gear," Mike called after me.

While going at an incredible speed I somehow managed to roll over on my stomach, inch my way up to the seat without falling off and put the brakes on. I felt like a stagecoach driver jumping onto a horse's back to save the passengers from a runaway team.

Well… O.K., the calf was probably only pulling it at about 10 yards per hour, but still, I could have fallen off and been seriously injured and the calf might have run through a fence or worse yet into a cow and made her mad before I got it stopped.

We finally got the calf doctored and as Mike took the rope off of its hind leg it stood quietly.

No sooner than I said, "Well, it looks like the calf finally decided we weren't the enemy after all," it reared up on its front legs and planted a well-placed kick to my thigh before bounding off to join the herd.

"I meant to tell you to watch out for the calf; it might kick," said Mike. "By the way what's for dinner?"

"Oh, yeah, I meant to tell you," I said. "We're going out for dinner…"

43

Plastic Earrings: The Rage In Calf Accessories

THERE ARE SEVERAL advantages to ear tagging calves. It helps identify which cow they came out of, gives you an easy way to record which calves have been doctored, and makes it easier to pick one out of a crowd, especially when they all look alike. You can say, "Oh, look at number 34; isn't he cute?"

Rather than having to say, "Oh, look at the one 40 feet from the 14th fence post on the south side of the pasture standing parallel to the barn with his mom who is the same color as the rest of the cows and has no unusual markings to make her stand out from the herd. Isn't he... oh, never mind, he moved."

Ear tagging gives a cow or calf an identity. Occasionally they lose their identity because it falls out or another cow steps on it when they are lying down. And since most cows have two ear tags, they still retain at least half of their identity.

There is one big disadvantage to ear tagging calves though — getting the tags in their ears. Contrary to people, who actually pay someone to poke holes in their ears, noses, belly buttons and other various body parts, calves don't seem to like it much. They run as fast as they can when they see us coming with the ear tagger. In fact, when you try to explain to them that plastic earrings are all the rage in calf accessories, they seem to understand the "rage" part, but little else.

Ear taggers work like a pair of pliers, just one quick squeeze of the handles and it's over. We're not asking them to stay still while we numb their ears with ice cubes, place a potato behind it and poke a hole through with a large, hot sewing needle. It's a very quick process, and would take less than two seconds if they would just cooperate.

We had one calf the other day that my husband, Mike, walked up behind and grabbed the hind foot with a calf catch. A calf catch is a long aluminum pole with a hook on the end that allows you to catch a critter from about 10 feet away. Needless to stay the calf didn't like the idea much and was well on his way to trying out for bucking rodeo stock.

Mike had inched his hands down the pole to within about three feet of the critter, but couldn't get a hold of the thrashing calf. He yelled to me to grab the end of the pole behind him to hold the calf's foot so he could let go long enough to grab the calf by the head. I soon discovered that grabbing the end of a long pole that is moving up and down and sideways, flaying uncontrollably as the calf hops around on three legs, is harder than it looks. That pole nearly beat me senseless about the head. I was close to developing cauliflower ears like the professional boxers do from getting hit too many times before I finally managed to get hold of it. Once I finally did latch onto it, it became pretty apparent — probably by the sight of me being drug around the field at the end of a ten-foot pole by the adrenaline high calf — that I wasn't going to be able to hold it for long.

Mike chased us down and threw his arms around the calf's neck and we came to a screeching halt.

"O.K.," he said, "Drop the pole and come up here and hold the calf so I can tag it."

I let go of the bar, which gave me a parting whack on the back of the head, and did as I was instructed.

I wrapped my arms around the calf's neck putting my whole body into it and waited... nothing happened.

"How do you expect me to tag him if you have his ears covered?" Mike said.

So I straddled the calf between my legs and hung on around its chest — that didn't work. The squirming calf almost got away.

The calf and I wrestled around some more until we finally fell to the ground. I soon found out that calves can kick almost as hard lying on their sides as they can standing up. As I was fending off the thrashing hooves like a seasoned Kung Fu fighter, I felt the hot breath of a mad cow sniffing my backside. Before I had a chance to wonder if the cow was going to flatten me, one of the calf's flaying hooves hit her on the nose. The cow shook her head and snorted before going back to a nearby pile of hay to commiserate with the other cows about how her own kid socked her in the snout.

I knew how she felt; I had about had it with her kid, too.

But Mike reminded me that if I kept messing around the calf would get away and we would never be able to catch it again.

So with my last ounce of strength I threw my body on the calf and pinned it to the ground. All those years of watching Saturday Night Wrestling finally paid off. Mike waded through the panting heap of tangled legs, arms and hooves, until he finally managed to find the calf's ears and tag them.

I let the calf up and rather than running, he just stood there next to me leaning against my legs. After all that fussing and fighting to try and get out of having his ears tagged, I couldn't figure out why he didn't take off. Then I looked over at the herd and there stood his mother shaking her head and bellowing at him. In cow language I'm pretty sure she was saying something like, "You get over here, young man, right this minute!" Only now she could call him by his full name, "Number Fourteen." When mom calls you by your full name that always translates to "You're in big trouble now!"

44

Hackin' and Whackin' The Bristled Thistle

THISTLES ARE A rancher's proverbial thorn in the side, and in the finger, and occasionally the ankle and sometimes the butt...The son of a biscuits are everywhere and multiply faster than zucchini on a hot day.

I've taken down a thistle or two or three during my years on the ranch, but this is the first year I've been placed on thistle patrol. As such I am a Private First Class of the Broadleaf Battalion and my husband is my self-appointed Commander in Chief. The only privileges a Private First Class gets on our ranch is a break for lunch, because the Private has to make it for the Commander, and a new shovel.

When he first ordered, I mean asked, me to accept this weed-fraught mission, I had reservations, but the lure of that shiny new shovel was just too tempting. He dangled it in front of me with the sharpened blade gleaming like he was enticing me with a diamond necklace.

"See how pretty and shiny it is," he said. "It will be all yours and no one else will be able to use it."

Wow, my very own shovel! I was so excited I had to go in the house and contemplate this new development while scrubbing the toilet, coincidently with my very own brush, which no one else is apparently able to use either.

I decided the exercise would do me good, and after all, how hard could it be to chop down a few thistles? I emerged from the house a short time later ready to thump on some thistles, but my shiny new shovel that had been ceremoniously propped up against the porch by my Commander was no where to be found.

I searched around the yard, in the shop, next to the driveway and couldn't find it anywhere. I was just about to give up when the Commander pulled into the driveway.

"I can't find my new shovel," I said as he stepped out of the pickup.

"Oh, I think I may have seen it down by the barn," he said somewhat reluctantly.

I started off to the barn, but remembered that I had left my gloves in the pickup earlier that day so turned back just in time to see the Commander dragging my shiny new shovel out from under a pile of irrigation tarps in the back of the pickup.

"By golly, look what I found," he said feigning surprise when he saw me approach. "I wonder how it got in there?"

I stood before him with my arms crossed giving him the ranch wife's stink eye, a kind of half squinted sideways look that we normally develop within the first year of marriage.

"Oh, my gosh," I said rather sarcastically as I grabbed the shovel, "it must have taken a flying leap right out of your hands and into the truck."

"Yeah, imagine that," he grinned.

I headed out for the nearest thistle, while glaring at him, but since it's hard to walk and give the ranch wife's stink eye at the same time, I eventually had to let it go or fall on my face.

"Make sure you get those in the far pasture next to the road when you're through up here," he called after me.

Puddin' Head, our black lab, Lord only knows what cross, was bouncing around with me as I became a human weed whacker. After about 40 minutes I had eradicated every thistle within a 100-yard radius of the yard fence and decided that this wasn't too bad a job after all. "Why does everyone make such a big deal of hackin' and whackin' a few thistles?" I wondered.

"Well, Puddin'," I said looking at my watch, "if we hurry and get those down by the road, we'll make it back just in time to watch Oprah." Puddin' always gets excited about watching Oprah. I don't like to watch it myself, of course; I just like to keep the dog happy.

As we approached the pasture near the road, I could hardly believe my eyes. In sharp contrast to the three or four dozen thistles we had just chopped down in the upper pasture, there were bazillions of them here! "Alrighty, so this is why thistles are such a big deal," I told Puddin'.

Scattered along the hillside like an invading army they stood waving in the breeze taunting me. Puddin' and I were completely outnumbered even with a new shovel.

"This will take forever," I told Puddin'.

She looked up at me whining sympathetically.

"Oh well," I said to her, "it's not like Oprah even has a last name; I guess this is more important."

I pried, pummeled and poked thistle after thistle. I became one with the shovel, literally. I had gripped the shovel so long and so hard that my hands wouldn't un-grip to let go of it. What seemed like forever, actually it was about 30 minutes and a sock full of stickers later, I decided it was time to call for reinforcements.

I whipped out my cell phone and called the Commander.

"Have you seen how many thistles are down here?" I said. "There's no way I can chop all of these down before they go to seed."

"Are you sure you're not just wanting to go watch Oprah?" he asked.

"No, good grief!" I said. "There's just too many of them. Couldn't I cut them down with the swather or something?"

"Well, there is one thing," he said, "that might be a little easier — chemical warfare."

"You mean…" I started to ask.

"Yes," he interrupted, "2, 4-D. But you will still have to get the big ones with a shovel. They don't respond as well to 2, 4-D as the little ones."

"Just how big is big?" I asked.

"Anything over about 16 inches," he replied.

After a quick survey of the area, I determined that everything was under 16 inches. Of course I didn't have a ruler on me, but heck I knew they were at least all under three feet and that seemed close enough — give or take a couple of inches.

So I returned to the base and came back outfitted with a four-wheeler and a tank full of chemical. Puddin' got to stay home this time to avoid getting sprayed — lucky dog got to watch Oprah after all.

I rode through the weeds astride the four-wheeler like a cowgirl in a western movie shooting vermin thistle on all sides with a 2,4-D spray gun. The bristled thistle began to recoil. If they had legs they would have run for their lives, because they were no match for me and my chemical-equipped Honda.

Even with this time saving technique, it was still three hours later when I pulled up in the driveway weary from battle.

I informed the commander that I had the enemy on the run and they were wilting fast.

He said, "Good job, Private. Tomorrow you can go back and chop down the big ones with a shovel."

"But..." I started to protest until he gave me the rancher's stink eye, which is similar to the rancher wife's stink eye, only really not fair at all.

"O.K.," I conceded, but first there is something I have to do."

What's that?" he said.

"I need to go get some spray paint so I can give my shovel a pink handle so no one else will be tempted to use it."

A rancher/rancher's wife stink eye stare off ensued...

45

Dial 1-800-Bad-Calf

WE DON'T TALK about it much, but nine out of 10 ranch wives are physically abused. I know those numbers are shocking, but I suspect it is even higher than that. The 10th woman is either abused and not fessing up or is still on her honeymoon and hasn't had to run calves up the chute yet.

We try not to complain, we always hope the next time it will be different, that the calves will somehow see the error in their ways and go calmly up the chute without kicking and stomping and head-butting the heck out of us. But it is never different...

My neighbor, Bev, says that abuse by calves has gotten so bad on their ranch that she has to wear dark pantyhose to hide the bruises on her legs when she wears a dress. And just about the time the bruises heal, it's time to wrestle another calf up the chute.

Most of us have tried many different tactics to stop the abuse. I've found one way to avoid being kicked by a calf is to stand as close to its rear end as possible. That way the calf doesn't have enough room to wind up for a really hard kick. This however, presents another problem – next to a calf's rear end is not a pleasant place to be. Just about the time I think I've escaped being kicked, the calf will poop. This, of course, causes me to jump back to avoid getting splattered and gives the calf the distance it needs to wind up and kick me square in the shin. Ranch wives commonly refer to this as the old "poop and punt" trick.

Calves have another trick, which they perform often, where they run past you at full speed and give you a little sideways kick. We call this the dash and poop, because let's face it, they are always pooping. This doesn't hurt as much as the full contact kick you get standing behind them, but it's enough of an impact to cause a bruise.

Even if by some miracle we avoid getting kicked hard while working calves, the largest calf in the herd inevitably decides to practice the Flamingo dance on our feet. It can't be satisfied with just a few little stomps. It has to perform the entire dance routine — the only thing missing is the guitar player and the castanets. Thus, and rightly so, this is referred to as the "poop and prance."

One thing I learned early on is to never bend over around a calf. They interpret your available backside as an invitation to practice their head butting skills. One time after being kicked by a calf in the chute, I bent over to rub my shin and the calf behind me butted me. It wasn't too hard, but it threw me off balance enough that I hit my head on the side of the chute and fell getting covered in mud and Lord only knows what else.

Which reminds me, the safety equipment industry has completely neglected ranch wives. I have never seen a helmet, padded clothing, special boots or any kind of strap or guard made for ranch wives who push calves up the chute. However, give a man a football, baseball or a hockey puck, and a multi- million dollar protective gear manufacturing business is born.

Due to the lack of support offered ranch wives in situations when they are exposed to abuse by a calf, I've often thought of starting a hotline, 1-800-bad-calf. Ranch wives could call to get the straight poop on what to do when they are a victim of abusive calves.

Caller: "Hello, bad calf hotline? I just can't take it any more. One calf kicked me five times today before I managed to get him in the head catch. To make matters worse, I have to work calves again today and I have to go to a dinner party tomorrow tonight and would like to wear a dress. Is there anyway to avoid getting kicked again so my legs aren't completely black and blue?"

Bad Calf: "I see your problem, but unfortunately, there is no way to prevent calves from being abusive at this time. I would suggest that you call Bev and ask her where she buys her bruise concealing pantyhose."

46

The Weaning

WE WEANED OUR calves last week and are still suffering from calf lag, which is similar to jet lag, but you don't get to go anywhere.

Over the years we have tried separating the calves from the cows first thing in the morning in hopes that by nightfall they would be settled down a little. We've also tried separating them late in the day in hopes that they wouldn't get too upset until the next day. But it doesn't seem to matter much because inevitably they decide the best time to really let loose and complain is just as we are about to fall asleep.

This year I even tried reasoning with our cows and calves. I told the cows to look at the bright side: their kids were out of the pasture, no more cleaning up after them, no more round the clock feedings, and they no longer had to find a babysitter when they wanted to go off into the far corners of the field to be alone.

I talked to the calves and told them they were now free to do anything they wanted without being reprimanded by their moms. They could stay up late, sleep in late, eat grass until they were bloated and butt heads to their heart's content. Heck, I even told them now that they were weaned they could get a tattoo branded on their sides and their ears pierced with square tags just like the adults.

Needless to say the calves weren't very responsive. They just stood there and looked at me like I was flapping my jaws in the wind and making nonsensical noises, similar to my own son, who by the way does not get the same branding and tattooing privileges.

The weaning always starts off slow with a couple of calves

bawling, which in turn gets a few cows bellowing and before long the whole herd is engaged in a pasture-wide moo- a-thon. There are times in the middle of the night when they give up for a few moments, but they have a backup system. During those momentary lapses as they rest their moo-chords, the cows have apparently entered into an agreement with the elk to ensure that we don't get any sleep. (Come to think of it this agreement is probably why the cows allow the elk to come in and eat our pastures forcing us to buy more hay — if you'll help us make noise all night for a week, we'll let you have the best clover.)

The minute our cows stop mooing, the cow elk start squealing on cue almost as if there is a bovine maestro waving a baton at the different animal orchestra sections to let them know when to start and how loud to wail. I suspect that while the elk are squealing, our cows are all standing around the water trough wetting their whistles and practicing their moo scales (moo, ray, me) preparing for their next musical set of the Cowharmonic led by Maestro Angus No. 43.

I've tried to tone down the elk section some during weaning nights by banging two pan lids together, but apparently the orchestra is not in need of a pajama clad cymbal ensemble as they pretty much ignore me.

After a few fitful hours of wrapping pillows around our ears and tossing and turning trying to sleep through the noise, there is at least somewhat of a reprieve. The cows stop mooing, the calves stop bawling and the elk stop squealing all at the same time. This is only however because the Maestro waves his baton at the soprano section — the coyotes. Once they start howling, our dog, Puddin' Head, recognizes her cue in this A Cappella musical and performs a solo from the front porch.

Finally on about the fifth night at about 2 a.m., the all- animal orchestra, which by then has included a few guest appearances in the form of caterwauling felines, comes to an end. And then, I bolt upright in bed, "What's that?" I ask my husband who was also stirred from his sleep aided by my kicking him in the shins.

"I don't know," he says as we both strain our ears in the darkness to hear. There's nothing... it's absolutely silent for the first time in almost a week. Yet we keep straining to hear this nothing that woke us up as if it were in itself a noise...

After a few minutes a little sound begins to pierce the darkness. As it begins to grow louder and louder we recognize it as our old friend the croaking toad who sits below our bedroom window crooning on cool fall nights.

"Whew," I let out a sigh of relief. "For a minute there I thought it was quiet."

"Yeah, that was kind of creepy," he says.

47

Smacking the Bulls in the Hood

I'VE FINALLY FIGURED out why bulls are called "bulls" – it's because they are bullies. They are always picking on some cow (no wonder cows get so mad), someone, something or each other. If bulls were allowed in the schoolyards, they would be the ones shaking you down every day for your lunch money and giving you wedgies.

We have one bull that is about four years old, and he has been ruler of the pastures this year because of his large size. Our 2-year old bulls have tried to take him on, but it's like watching a Volkswagen Beetle collide with a Hummer – you know which one is going to stay on the road and which one is going to get shoved into the ditch before it even happens.

The reign of power shifted this week when the older bull ended up lame. We don't have any idea how it happened, but he somehow injured his shoulder and can barely walk. The 2-year olds took advantage of his weakness and formed an alliance like some kind of Bulls in the Hood gang, and together beat up on the older bull. The older bull stood his ground, but after each encounter, and there were several a day, it was obvious his shoulder was getting worse.

This presented a problem because the older bull was too far out in the pasture to get him to a corral because he could barely stand, much less walk, and it was obvious he couldn't or wouldn't climb into a livestock trailer without a great deal of assistance.

My husband and I discussed several ways to get him out of the pasture and away from the Bulls in the Hood including haltering him and hooking a come-along to it to ratchet him up a makeshift ramp into the trailer. We thought I could also give him a little incentive from behind by pushing his butt with my Subaru. We discounted that idea though because similar to an age-old riddle, "Where does a 2,000- pound bull sit?" Anywhere he wants to — and in this case it would probably be on the hood of my Subaru.

Short of hiring a helicopter to lift him or hoisting him onto a flatbed with a crane, we finally decided the best plan of action would be to leave him where he is and build an electric fence around him to the keep the young bulls out. "Brilliant idea!" you say. Yes, we thought so, but there was still the problem of keeping the Bulls in the Hood away from him while we erected the fence, which would take several hours.

Since the National Guard would probably think defending the country was a little more important than defending our bull, we decided my husband would put up the fence while I became the bull's bodyguard.

I armed myself with my weapon of choice, a shovel, mainly because I always seem to have one in my hands anyway, and stood by the bull's side waiting for the attack from the Hood. It didn't take long.

Just as I was in mid chorus of "Bad bulls, bad bulls, whatcha gonna do..." two young bulls came charging across the pasture bellowing some kind of bovine war cry and skidded to a stop about 20 feet away. They proceeded toward the big guy and me with a kind of lopsided shoulder first, head down walk that was their way of showing they meant business. Again, if they had been bullies in the schoolyard, they would have been punching their fists into their open hands trying to intimidate us.

I stepped in front of the old bull, raised my shovel and gave my best "Cowabunga" yell. The two young bulls turned and ran.

"See, it's just that easy," I said to the old bull. In return, he snorted at me. Unfortunately, the young bulls interpreted that snort as a challenge and came galloping back.

"Now look what you've done," I told the old bull. He just blinked his eyes and shrugged his good shoulder as he braced himself for a fight.

This time the two were not buying my Cowabunga routine and

did not retreat. I hopped up and down, called them names and told them I'd tell their rancher on them, but they kept advancing. One of them lowered his head and tried to get around me to the old bull so I smacked him square on the forehead with the flat side of the shovel. He spun around bucking, bellowing and running, fortunately away from me.

In the meantime, the other bull had tried to attack the old bull from behind so I turned and smacked him on the head as well. They both ran off to soothe their injured egos and stood a short distance away, looking at me as if to say, "How could you?"

This repeated charging, shovel smacking, and retreating went on for over an hour.

I finally yelled over to my husband, "If I'm going to have to keep this up much longer, I'll need a cape, red boots and gold wristbands." He turned and flashed a big grin at me. "No," I said, "I was just kidding. I'm not going to dress up like Wonder Woman for you."

Now would be a good time to point out that my husband was less than 20 yards away during all of this. I probably wouldn't have hit a bull on the head with anything without knowing I could run over and stand behind him if one of the bulls were to become incensed at my shovel smacking and retaliate. You always need to have a good buffer handy — or at the very least someone you can run faster than — when you start smacking bulls.

The old bull soon tired of standing. I'm not sure why, because it's not like he had to actually do anything during this whole ordeal, but he decided to lie down. As soon as he stretched out on the ground the two young bulls meandered back out into the pasture to graze with the rest of the herd.

"That's it," I said to the old bull. "All you have to do is lie down and they go away? Couldn't you have thought of that a little sooner?" After all I had done to protect him he just closed his eyes and sighed like I was a pesky, noisy little fly on his backside.

48

Sledding Calf and the Creature from the Swamp

CALVING IN TWO feet of snow has been a challenge this year, especially for our first time heifers. They seem to have the natural instinct that tells them to seek out a somewhat secluded location to give birth to their four-legged bundles of joy, but I don't think calving on the side of an icy hill is what the creator had in mind.

Somewhere along their neurotransmitter lines, the message starts out as "find a suitable location" and ends up something like "just park it anywhere, sister." The highest snowdrift, the slickest slab of ice or the deepest irrigation ditch they can find are apparently all within their realm of great places to have a baby.

To top it off they cross their legs and hold on to that baby until they sense an impending blizzard and then wait until the snow and wind are at their peak. I think they also stick a hoof in their mouths and hold it up to check the direction of the wind and make sure they position themselves so it is blowing directly on the emerging calf.

We had one heifer that tried in earnest to calve on a 20- foot glacier and finally gave up. My husband, Mike, and I herded her to the barn and tried to get her into a nice clean stall that we had prepared with straw bedding. No amount of coaxing or pushing could convince her to go into the stall. Instead she lay down in the barn's alleyway and plopped her offspring onto the dirt floor.

Once the wet, slimy calf came to life it started flopping around in the dirt and as it tried to stand up, it looked like some creature rising from the swamp in a horror movie. The heifer took one look at the mud-caked youngster and ran into the stall, the stall that only moments before we couldn't make her go in to.

Since it was obvious the heifer wasn't going to get much

accomplished on her own, I began cleaning off and drying the calf while Mike went to check the other heifers. By this time it was midnight, the snow was blowing and the wind was howling.

Another heifer had calved in the field on a pile of snow and the calf had gotten too cold and couldn't get up. We brought it into the house and dried it off with hair dryers and electric heaters, but it was too weak to stand. We decided to leave it under the pile of blankets next to the stove and go lay down on the couch and get some sleep.

At 2 a.m., we are really not at our best and having each other's feet in our faces as we struggled to get comfortable in our insulated Carhartts didn't help much. The first hour was taken up with complaints like "you're kneeing me in the back," "you're laying on my elbow," and "get your toe out of my nose." In spite of this we somehow managed to drift off to sleep anyway.

Just as I was getting used to the smell of wool socks that had spent the last 12 hours sweating in a pair of Sorrell snow boots the sun rose over the couch and it was time to get up. We got the calf up, managed to get a little milk down him and then took him outside to find his mother.

You've probably heard the saying, "Absence makes the heart grown fonder." With heifers, absence seems to make them forget because the heifer acted like she had no idea whose baby this was that we were shoving in front of her nose.

We decided to put them in the barn where they could be confined and get reacquainted. We got the heifer in a stall next to the other heifer with her swamp thing and went back to get the calf.

Getting the heifer to the barn, which is down a hill from our house and the pasture where we calve out the heifers, was not too difficult. Getting the calf that was too weak to walk very far was another matter.

The calf was too big to carry that far and had just enough fight in him that he wouldn't cooperate. As we mulled over our options I spied the kid's snow sled that we had sitting in the yard.

I'm not sure if it was a good idea or if we were just so tired it made sense, but we put the calf on the sled and launched him down the hill toward the barn. The idea was that we would run along side the sled and make sure he didn't fall off, but the sled was some kind of purple racer rocket and it went faster than we could keep up in the deep snow. All we could do was watch as the calf zoomed down the hill with his ears blown back and his nose in the air.

Miraculously the calf leaned from side to side with the dips and turns of the sled and managed to stay on. He reached the bottom of the hill, got off the sled and shook his head, slightly dazed from the adventure. The ride seemed to have invigorated him though and this time when we put him with his mother, the heifer didn't have the option of acting like she didn't know him. After a ride like that I guess he figured he was entitled to the "Breakfast of Champions."

49

Defending the Grass

IT WAS A dark and stormy night. I had just slipped off into a deep slumber — a deep, snoreless slumber (contrary to what my husband says, I don't snore) — when two shots rang out piercing the silence.

I bolted upright in bed. I sat and listened. Other than a coyote howling in the distant hills, the night was silent. That is if you don't count the gentle hum of the computer downstairs, the constant revving of the refrigerator, and the bulls bellowing in the pasture. And, oh yeah, a dark and stormy night tends to make a little racket too.

But, still, everything seemed normal, so I lay back down and just as I dozed off again — kaboom, kaboom!

This time I knew it wasn't my snoring...er, ah, I mean the storm, so I reached over and flipped on the bedside lamp. I immediately noticed that my husband had pushed all of the blankets over to my side of the bed. He does that pretty often although he has a funny name for his generosity. He calls me a "bed hog." Oh, and a few minutes later I also noticed that he wasn't in the bed. I'm pretty observant that way.

I cautiously peered over the edge of the bed to see if I had accidentally kicked him onto the floor in my sleep, again.

Before I could get my head back up from over the edge of the bed, I heard it again — kaboom, kaboom. Now that I was wide-awake, it was so loud it startled me and I whacked my head on the edge of the nightstand.

This time I could tell the noise was coming from outside. I crawled out of bed and looked out the window. I gasped at what I saw. It was truly a sight that dark and stormy nights are known for. There in the moonlight stood a man in a trench coat and rubber boots holding a rifle!

"Oh my gosh," I thought. "There's a dangerous criminal, probably a pervert or Lord only knows what else, lurking right outside our bedroom window and my husband, and supposedly my protector, is nowhere around."

As my eyes struggled to focus into the darkness the shape standing in the field began to look vaguely familiar. It wasn't a trench coat, it was a bathrobe, and the boots were of the irrigating variety. O.K. the mystery of my husband's disappearance was solved – he was the dangerous criminal/ pervert standing in the field.

But what in the heck was he doing? He pointed the shotgun into the air and fired, kaboom, kaboom.

"Egad," I thought, "he's trap shooting using the stars as targets instead of clay pigeons!"

I threw open the window. "I know you need all the practice you can get," I yelled, "but for crying out loud, can't you shoot at the stars some other time — some other time...oh I don't know... besides midnight!"

Kaboom, Kaboom!

Having received such a rude response, I slammed the window shut and went back to bed.

A few minutes later he walked into the bedroom.

"For your information, I wasn't shooting at the stars, I was trying to scare the elk away before they eat all of the cow pasture," he said rather irritated.

"Oh, sorry," I said. "Usually you do that in your underwear with pots and pans. The rubber boots and the trench coat threw me."

"Trench coat?" he asked.

"Never mind," I said.

We're going on our fifth night now of shooing somewhere around 100 head of elk out of the pasture.

I say "we" even though I'm not actually the one running around in the middle of the night with a shotgun, because I'm suffering the sleep deprivation side effects from it. The elk hazing doesn't happen at the same time every night, but it's always "after" I get to sleep.

My husband can be sound asleep on the couch with the TV blaring, while the neighbors are visiting with him, and when the dog is hocking up something dead in the middle of the living room floor, but one little far off squeal of a cow elk and he jolts awake faster than a teenager on an energy drink. It doesn't even have to be a full squeal. It can be an elk hiccup a mile away and he's armed and ready to defend his grass!

He started out by sneaking up on the elk, while they were all standing by the fence peering into the pasture watching him. Pretty soon though they got to where they were coming in closer every night and weren't far enough away to sneak up on. So he began defending the area from our yard. It's a good thing we don't have wagons or I'm sure we would have to circle them every night before going to bed.

And even though I know it's going to happen sometime in the middle of the night, and he says I should be used to it by now, every time it does, for some reason, unbeknownst to my husband, I just can't seem to sleep through the sound of a double barrel shotgun going off right outside the bedroom window.

I told my husband at breakfast this morning that I'm going to check into a sleep center.

"That's a good idea," he said. "Maybe they can do something about your snoring."

"No, I mean so I can get some sleep," I said. "And for the last time, I don't snore!"

"What do you think wakes me up every night?" he said. "I use your snoring as an alarm to get up to listen for the elk. It works pretty good during calving season too."

I'm thinking I just might have one of those episodes tonight where I "accidentally" kick him over the edge of the bed while I'm asleep...and I think he's going to be very generous with the blankets!

50

The Feng Shui Ranch

I RECENTLY READ a book on Feng Shui and how to "create your sacred space." Feng Shui is the ancient Chinese practice of the placement and arrangement of space, including things that take up space, to achieve harmony with the environment. Apparently when your space is properly positioned, you will be receptive to good fortune.

It was quite interesting and it got me to wondering how Feng Shui principles could be applied on the ranch. So I told my husband that we needed to assess "our space" and see if we were in balance.

"We probably should," he said, "but I don't want to."

Since the burden of determining if we are in balance was left up to me, I started with what I thought was a logical area, the barn. The book says that the area surrounding the entrance should be completely clear. So I picked up a couple of buckets sitting outside near the barn door that we use to grain the young bulls. Keeping in mind that the book says, if you have to have clutter keep it off the ground, I hung them on a nail inside a stall in the barn.

Next, there was a stack of salt block trays that I neatly placed inside the stall out of sight along with a few livestock whips.

This stall was quickly becoming what the book described as a "junk room." Junk rooms, the book says, will have a negative impact on some area of your life. Since I couldn't figure out what area of my life was being negatively affected by a junk stall, I decided it was O.K. to have one and proceeded to put several more things in it. After all that clutter has to go somewhere if we are going to achieve my goal of having a Feng Shui Ranch.

Inside the barn, various items such as halters, hotshots, ropes, covered barrels full of cat food, grain and oats, syringes and medicines lined the walls and floor. Wow, this barn is just full of clutter I thought to myself. No wonder our flow of energy is restricted. It's not that we are getting older after all; our Feng is just out of sync with our Shui. So I gathered up everything that wasn't nailed down and shoved it into the junk stall.

I briefly wondered if clutter also included dried up cow poop, but quickly decided that since it's organic material, it could be considered part of the ground, rather than something on the ground, and could remain where it was.

Satisfied that I had achieved the proper balance in the barn, I went outside and looked around at other areas that might need to be cleared of negative energy.

I spotted a cow that was standing in the corrals and wondered if she would benefit from space clearing. The book says moving a person's energy can help clear out negative feelings. Since this cow had been kind of ornery when we gave her a shot the day before, I thought it might be worth a try.

As I approached her, I tried to sense her electromagnetic energy by waving my hands gently through the air. When I thought I felt a little tingling sensation, I tried to engage her energy so I could move out her negative vibes and replace them with positive ones. I wasn't sure which direction to move the energy so I tried moving it to the left and the right. As it turns out that tingling sensation I felt, I suspect is similar to the one that people get just before lightning strikes them. The cow did not respond well to having her energy moved, so she used all of that negative energy she had bottled up to run me out of the corral.

I was somewhat confused because I had read that in some countries, the cow is considered to be a sacred animal that represents good fortune. (I'm suspecting that this is probably where the term "holy cow" originated.) In fact, a cow seated on a pile of gold ingots is believed to be a very potent Feng Shui symbol. But since we don't happen to have a pile of gold lying around, and I doubt that we could get a cow to sit on it anyway, I will just have to take the writer's word for it.

After that encounter, I decided that cows must have their own way of attaining Feng Shui. If you get in their space, they will clear you out! So I decided to leave the cows alone for now and go back to the house and move some energy and dust around with the vacuum cleaner. A few hours later, my husband came dragging himself into the house just exhausted.

"What's wrong?" I asked.

"Well, I got a cow out of the back pasture and managed to get her all the way up to the barn to give her a shot for foot rot and couldn't find the medicine or syringes," he said as he collapsed on the couch. "I had her in the chute, but couldn't make her go forward into the head catch because I couldn't find the hotshot. Then the bulls in the pen next to us got excited and started running around getting her upset so I thought I would toss them a little grain to quiet them down, while I looked for the medicine. But I couldn't find the buckets or the grain. The cats were pawing all over me in the barn wanting to be fed, but I couldn't even find the dang cat food."

"Then, to make matters worse," he continued, "that cow we got in yesterday to give a shot charged me when I went into the corral. I don't know what the heck her problem is. She's never done that before."

"Oh, my gosh!" I said, trying to sympathize with his plight and nonchalantly sneak out of the room.

"Wait a minute," he said, now on his feet with his hands on hips looking directly at me. "You wouldn't happen to know anything about all of this, would you?"

Sensing that this would not be a good time to try to move his energy, I told him about my efforts to achieve harmony and balance on the ranch.

Needless to say I am banned from trying to move a cow's energy in any direction, and now I know why a junk stall/room can have a negative impact on my energy. By the time I got everything moved back to where it was supposed to be, I was pooped!

51

Great Galloping Heifers!

I GET A kick out of working baby calves through the chute. Seriously, I do, they kick me every chance they get. In spite of their lower limb jabs and hooks though, they aren't very big and can't do much damage to my shins. In fact I enjoy being around them so I always jump at the chance to help with the little buggers. That's why when my husband asked me to help him work the heifer calves a few weeks ago I didn't have any qualms about it whatsoever.

Being the nice guy that he is, my husband warned me that these calves were a little larger than the ones I was used to helping him with, and he graciously volunteered to call one of his friends to help if I didn't think I could handle it. Now, I don't know about other ranch wives, but asking me if I can handle it — them's fighting words. You better believe I can handle it! And on the outside chance that I can't, I will never admit it!

So fortified with too much pride and several peanut butter cookies I marched out to the corrals this cold November day with my Carhartt overalls on and my hackles up. As we began herding the 8-month-old heifers from the feed bunk into the corrals I immediately noticed something odd. For some reason when calves are out in the pasture running around, they look much smaller than when they are standing next to you. Good grief, I thought to myself, these critters are just a few short months and a half dozen head butts from becoming full- grown cows. And, as I soon discovered, they were each about 500 pounds of pure stubbornness, a trait passed on from their equally uncooperative mothers.

My job, the one I always volunteer for with the baby calves, was to run each heifer up the chute because although they were bigger, they were still small enough that they could turn around in the chute. My husband worked the head catch and a local veterinarian, Mark, bangs (brucellosis) vaccinated the heifers because a legal record and identification number of it is required. I used to think that bangs vaccinations were what gave cows their stylish haircuts, but have since learned that it prevents a disease called brucellosis.

I was a little concerned about the size of these critters, but the first heifer ran right up the chute at a full gallop with hardly any prodding from me — that is until she came to the head catch. The minute her nose touched the opening she put on her brakes and skidded to a stop on the muddy ground. Since I was running behind her and didn't expect her to stop I almost rear-ended her. And believe me, rear-ending a heifer of any size is a very smelly proposition. She immediately turned around and forced her way past me. There really wasn't enough room for both of us to stand side by side so she squeezed me flat like an almost empty tube of toothpaste and stepped on my foot on her way by.

This was about the time it crossed my mind that I really wished people could be smashed flat and then pop up unscathed ready to run again like a cartoon character. But, since I didn't have that capability, and two men were waiting at the head catch for my next amazing feat, I hobbled down the chute after her mumbling the same words that made Bugs Bunny famous – "Of course, you realize, this means war!"

I maneuvered her down the chute again at a full gallop, and just like before she skidded to a stop before entering the head catch, only this time I was prepared and grabbed her head and pushed it forward before she could manage to turn around. After what seemed like hours, probably two minutes in reality, and much poking, prodding and pushing on my part she finally stepped into the head catch.

The next few used the same method — galloping up the chute, skidding to a stop and trying to turn around — but just as I was getting down a routine, a gargantuan heifer came through. She was used to throwing her weight around and not quite as timid as the others. Like the other heifers though she galloped up the chute and skidded to a stop, but rather than trying to turn around, she backed up. By then the muddy ground in the chute had turned into a combination of regular mud stuff mixed with heifer natural fertilizer stuff and was so slick I couldn't get any traction. Despite my best efforts of using my body as a human roadblock, she shoved me all the way back down the chute like a cross country skier with an 80-mile an hour tail wind.

I prodded her into the chute again, and as I was running behind her yelling, poking and flapping my arms, I slipped in the muddy slime and fell down. Fortunately my flailing around in the mud and crud like a wounded flamingo scared her enough that she kept going forward, but once again, she skidded to a stop right before entering the head catch.

I learned a long time ago that the closer you stand to a calf's back end, as unpleasant as that is, the harder it is for them to kick you. They can't get enough distance between you and their foot to really let you have it. And after I managed to stand up I had enough slime on my Carhartts to star in an alien invasion movie so trying to avoid her bovine derrière was no longer a problem. I got a run at it and plowed into her similar to a football guard clearing a path for the quarterback. I lambasted her with everything I had — and she didn't budge an inch.

As the veterinarian and my husband continued coaxing me "come on, push, push, push, you can do it" I began to wonder which one of them would finally announce, "congratulations — it's a healthy, bouncing baby girl!"

After what seemed like an eternity of my shouting and shoving, the veterinarian finally leaned over the chute and gave her a little tickle with his fingers on her back. This little tickle for some reason, after my plowing into her upwards of 50 miles an hour, and slapping, yelling, prodding and elbowing her, doing everything except putting on a big bad wolf Halloween mask, startled her and she jumped right into the head catch.

There were only 25 heifer calves to work that day, but to justify the stiffness and soreness I suffered for days afterward, let's say there were at least 100 calves that I had to shove up the chute.

And while we're at it let's say I did this single- handedly through four feet of snow in the worst blizzard this area has ever had and the chute was situated on a 45-degree angle uphill, both ways. Oh, yeah — I can handle it!

52

Bottle Brats

FEEDING ONE CALF from a bottle is fun. Feeding more than one is like throwing yourself in a pond of piranhas and hoping you will make it out alive.

The calves will rush in and attack you from all sides trying to wrap their lips around everything from your shoelaces to your elbow. And when you tell them the milk is "all gone" they react similar to a 2-year-old child who has had his daily quota of sugar and wants more. All gone doesn't mean diddley squat to a screaming 2-year-old and likewise calves think you could surely come up with something if they just head butted you long enough and hard enough.

I fed two orphaned calves this year, "Tri" and "Tip." Tri was abused by his mother, a young heifer that kicked him every time he tried to have dinner, and Tip was a twin that was abandoned by her mother in favor of her larger brother. So you can see they both had "issues" coming into this new feeding relationship.

I helped them work through their anger and abandonment problems by providing them with knees, thighs and hips to head butt as well as toes to stomp on. After 10 minutes of messing me up good during feeding times, they always felt better about their situations.

They had a pretty good buddy system worked out similar to Demolition and the New Age Outlaws on WWE wrestling tag teams. While Tri would start rooting around at my behind, Tip would go for my armpit. It wouldn't matter that I had the bottles right in front of their faces, they would have to exhaust all other possibilities of where they thought milk might come from first.

Once they were satisfied that milk was not forthcoming from my pant leg, they finally latched on to the bottles' rubber udders.

For a glorious five seconds, they were totally content, sucking and gulping the milk down into their rumbling stomachs. The wonderful feeling of a baby animal leaning against your legs bonding with you is only surpassed by the wonderful feeling of getting the heck out of their pen before they attack again.

Unfortunately, two hungry calves can move faster than a middle-aged rancher after that last piece of cherry cobbler, so I seldom make it out before the head butting commences. Now that they know I can somehow provide the milk, they try and force more out of me with their foreheads. Usually all they get, however, is a few choice adjectives that I purposely save up for occasions such as this.

They always seem to manage to butt at least one of the bottles, which goes flying out of my hands. I learned very quickly, and I might add a little painfully, about the folly of bending over to pick up a dropped bottle. A rump in the air is like a butting beacon to a calf. In most cases it is the largest target in the vicinity and what he perceives is his best chance at making something happen. So I've actually become quite adept at kicking the bottle over the fence rather than picking it up because my ability to sit down again depends on it. I practice dropkicking and punting bottles in the yard year-around to hone my skills in anticipation of feeding calves.

If you, however, are not an accomplished bottle kicker, I would suggest taking off your shoe and picking the bottle up with your toes or make sure you have a large supply of extra bottles so you can just leave them laying in the calf pen — anything to avoid bending over.

You would think that after awhile the calves would realize that no amount of head butting to my backside is going to turn the milk spigot on and that kneecaps don't make good pacifiers.

After several months of having the calves decorate my body with black and blue marks and being drenched in calf slobber, I began to wonder who would be ideally suited to bottle feed calves. I think the Michelin Man and the Stay Puff Marshmallow

Man could be worthy contenders due to the extra padding they pack around. A sumi wrestler also comes to mind, as he would be hard for a couple of calves to push around. Wonder Woman could lasso the bottles with her golden rope and would never have to bend over...

But I guess when it comes right down to it, I still want to feed the calves myself because in spite of their head butting, slobbering and toe stomping, that split second that they look at me through long fluttering eyelashes as they wrap their necks around my legs and lean against me makes it all worthwhile..

53

Gun Fever

WHILE HAVING DINNER at a restaurant the other night, a friend of ours happened to mention that her guard dog, a Great Pyrenees/Akbash cross just had puppies. We were teeth deep into our steaks when she said to my husband, "You know, you guys could really use one of these dogs. You wouldn't ever have to worry about coyotes on your place again."

"I don't worry about coyotes now," said my husband. "I have a varmint rifle that sits by the door. I don't have to feed it; it only barks when I pull the trigger, and it doesn't poop."

"Which reminds me," he said as he turned to me.

I quickly tried to change the subject.

"Isn't this great flat iron steak?" I said. "Boy, what about those 49ers, I hear they're on a winning streak. Hey, did you know that farmers in England are required by law to provide their pigs with toys?"

But it was too late. His eyes were already glazing over and his upper lip was beginning to tremble with excitement. A faint layer of perspiration began to pool on his forehead and he was squinting down the upper tine of his fork drawing a bead on a bottle of Bud Light resting on a table across the restaurant.

"I could use another rifle," he said reluctantly letting the bottle slip from his fork sight as if to give the beer a reprieve. Fortunately he didn't get out the higher caliber steak knife or the double barrel spoon.

I ignored his comment hoping against all hope that he was merely having an intense craving for alcohol. But all the signs were there – the itchy trigger finger, the amnesia about how many guns he already owns, and incoherent babbling about how good the cattle market is expected to be this year. Yup, it was evident, he had gun fever.

Unfortunately, the only known cure for gun fever is to buy guns and the recommended dosage depends largely on the size of the pocketbook and how well the afflicted can ignore the resistance offered by his wife. However, I suspect the medical professional who came up with this remedy owns shares in Remington and Winchester companies.

We made it through dinner and when he began telling the waitress how he could shoot a two-inch twig off of a tree in a snowstorm with 60-mile an hour winds, blindfolded, if only he had the Remington 40XRBR with a 2 oz. trigger, custom stock and Nikon Monarch 5-20x44SF riflescope, I knew it was time to take him home.

As soon as we got in the car he started mapping out for me where "we" could get his rifle, the best person to buy the custom stock from and a great discount warehouse for scopes.

He continued with his tangent, which sounded something like blah, blah, blah, ammunition, blah, blah, blah, barrels, blah, blah, blah, bluing, bullets, blah, blah, blah, cases, cleaning, gauges, and blah, blah, gunpowder. To me it all translated in to something along the lines of "Let's take all of the money we have and invest it in a skink farm."

After the 30-minute drive home I was exhausted and beaten. Nothing I had said, not even, "You'll shoot your eye out!" had any affect on him. He was so delirious with the fever that he even began talking about getting two varmint rifles, so he would have one for 500 yards and one for 1,000 yards.

"You can't even see something as small as a varmint at 1,000 yards!" I protested.

"Hellllloooooo," he said, "that's why I've been telling you we need to get two of the Nikon Monarch 5-20x44SF rifle scopes."

"O.K.," I finally gave in, "get your new rifle."

That was immediately followed by a glaring stare from him, the same kind of look a well-seasoned boxer gives his opponent before knocking him out of the ring.

"O.K.," I said, "get your *two* new rifles."

"Really!" he said. "You don't mind?"

"No, go ahead. Just tell me about how much it will cost," I said.

"Well," he said as he started mentally figuring the price of the rifles, custom stocks, after market triggers, scopes and reloading equipment, "it could be as high as $4,000 for everything."

"Fine," I said as I grabbed a mug of hot cider and sat down in front of the computer with a stack of mail order catalogs.

"What are doing?" he asked.

"I figured I better get started because it's going to take me awhile to decide what I want to get for $4,000," I said.

"What do you mean?" he said with a puzzled look.

"Well, I'm sure you want to be fair, don't you?" I asked. "If you are spending $4,000, then I should be able to spend that much, too, shouldn't I?"

Miraculously, like the dark clouds opening to reveal the light of the sun, the fever began to break.

"You know," he said, "I guess I don't really need those rifles after all. I already have one that seems to be doing the job. Besides we need to buy fertilizer this spring for the pastures and we do have a pretty high gas bill to pay this month."

"Yeah," I said, "you're right. It's a good thing you are so sensible when it comes to money or we'd be in debt up to our ears."

He smiled and leaned over and kissed me on the forehead before trotting up the stairs to bed.

I immediately grabbed a pen and paper and began to draft the following letter:

Dear members of the American Medical Association:

I, a mere rancher's wife, have single-handedly discovered a cure for a malady that has affected men since the mid 1200s when man first discovered that lit gunpowder could project a stone through the air. Yes, incredulous as it may seem, I have found a cure for gun fever....

54

Bruised and Battered by Minerals

THERE WAS NO tornado, for once a cow didn't run over me, and I wasn't side swiped by a Volkswagen bus. Had one or any combination of those things happened to me, I would have at least had a good excuse for the battering I took last weekend that left me looking and feeling like I'd been prodded up the cattle chute five too many times.

Nope, I can't blame the beating I took from being in a natural disaster or even an unnatural one. I was physically abused by a 50-pound sack of livestock supplement. I know, as incredible as it may seem, I let a sack of highly palatable trace minerals and vitamins with the aroma cows love get the best of me.

One reason we are feeding our cows this supplement is because the sack says it is supposed to promote optimum body condition and reduce winter stress. I think they got it backwards because it actually reduced my body condition and promoted my optimum winter stress.

I picked up the unwieldy bag of minerals, which weighs almost half as much as me, and proceeded to take it out to the cows. I vaguely remember thinking, "I wonder why Mike, (my husband) had worn a path in the snow all along the edge of the fence to pack the minerals to the cows rather than cut across the middle of the field to the salt feeder?" Apparently, it was one of those thoughts where I decided I was just a little smarter than the average rancher and could save myself a few extra steps. I seem to have a lot of thoughts like that…

The snow was about two feet deep and had formed a hard crusty surface on top – or so I thought. I took about 10 steps and suddenly my feet went through the top layer of snow. I immediately fell to my hands and knees, and dropped the sack of minerals.

I was wearing insulated overalls, a down coat, heavy snow pack boots and thick mittens, which didn't allow much freedom of movement. I must have looked like a beached whale flopping around on the snow unable to bend at the knees and elbows. I finally wallowed around and made it back to my feet.

I have been told I'm stubborn and now I'm beginning to think there must be some truth to that, because I was even more determined to stay on the route that I had chosen rather than back up and follow the path already in place.

I tried it again, and again, and about every 10 steps I went through the top of the snow and fell to my knees dropping the bag of mineral.

I was so tired from repeatedly falling and picking up the bag that by the time I neared the feeder, I was on my belly pushing the bag across the snow in front of me. I had to flounder around on the ground with the bag for a good 10 minutes before I could muster the strength to lift it up completely over my head and into the feeder. Thank goodness the feeder is only about six inches off the ground or I never would have made it.

Fortunately, this mineral company makes their bags with a waterproof plastic coated lining. I'm guessing that must mean I'm not the only one to have wallowed one of their bags around in the snow. They must have crash test ranch wives, similar to the crash test dummies used in the auto industry to try out their products and determine what safety features are needed.

Unfortunately, although the bags are waterproof, it turns out those ranch wives doing the testing must have never tried to open the bags, or the company would have realized the need to come up with a better system. I have never pulled that stitched-in string at the top of a mineral bag or even a bag of dog food and had it work. Either the string breaks or it bunches into a knot. And yes, I've tried both ends and both sides. If the companies insist on using this method they need to attach a disposable seam ripper to every bag or at the least include a coupon to hire some help, perhaps the men who model for the covers of romance novels could use some extra work...

At any rate, this bag was no exception and after all the work of getting it to the feeder, I couldn't get it open. I dug through my pockets for a knife, but all I found was a hair barrette and a half eaten Ding Dong. I poked and prodded at the bag of minerals with my barrette until the barrette bent in two from the pressure, much like me.

I ripped at the bag with my fingernails, I kicked it with my boots, I cussed at it, but none of this helped, although the cussing did make me feel a little better. I scanned the pasture; there was no rock, stick or rodent in sight with large teeth so out of desperation I finally decided to gnaw on it myself.

I chewed on the bag like a rat after grain, and finally after several minutes, I managed to make a small hole, which I was able to enlarge enough with my fingers to finally spill out that precious mineral.

Yes, I had been battered and bruised by a bag of minerals, but on the bright side, after chewing the bag open, I'm pretty sure I don't have a selenium deficiency.

55

Bad Bart Gets the Boot

IF OUR BLACK Angus bull, Bart, were a person he'd be like one of those gun-slinging outlaws from the movies who could simultaneously shoot a man in the back while charming the ladies.

In his short life, he's nearly 2 years old, he has already gained a reputation on our place. When we turned him in with the cows and other bulls for the first time this summer he acted like the new guy in prison. He immediately went over to the biggest 4-year-old bull we have and head butted him. A fight ensued, and what Bart lacked in size and experience he made up for in persistence. He eventually wore the other bull down until he tired of the struggle and walked away. Needless to say the cows swoon over him — the bulls avoid him.

Bart has the typical bad boy story. He started life as an orphan. He didn't know his father, he could have been any one of about 10 bulls and of course none of those bulls owned up to it. Shortly after birth his mom was taken away to another pasture by mistake, anyway that's what we were told. We have to wonder if perhaps his mother just left him for greener pastures and that's the story his previous owner told him to spare his feelings.

At some point Bart will probably have to go on the Montel Williams show or Oprah to find out who his true father is. As usually happens on those shows, I'm sure there will be a big scene with lots of denial on the dad's part — "she's out in the pasture with 10 other bulls, how do you know he's mine? Bart doesn't even look like me, he has a small head and beady eyes." And then there will be lots of crying when Bart's dad is backed into a corner and made to realize that the DNA tests don't lie, and he will have to start paying child support or in Bart's case, share some grass.

At any rate, Bart was smaller than the other bulls and obviously picked on during his first few months of life, as evidenced by his surly attitude. His smaller size, however is what attracted us to him, because being smaller, he was also cheaper.

We started feeding Bart grain when he was a youngster and thus got to know him quite well. He was corralled with another young bull, Bert. Every time we grained them Bart would spend about 15 minutes trying to run Bert away from the feed bunk. Consequently Bart grew like a weed since he was eating the amount of grain meant for two bulls. Bert unfortunately became an underachiever with low self-esteem and rather than go out into the pasture with the cows and be further subjected to Bart and the other bulls, he went to the livestock sale where he sold his body to the highest bidder — a sad, but all too common story.

When we were graining Bart, we made the mistake of scratching his back one day. After that, he insisted that we scratch it every day. He always started out nice, like a puppy wanting a pat on the head, but his mild demeanor always deteriorated rather rapidly. He would lower his head and place it against one of our knees. We thought, "how cute!" and would continue scratching.

His thoughts, however, were more along the lines of "Let me remind you who is in charge." After a few minutes of scratching, he would get this funny look in his eyes and cock his head sideways similar to the way John Wayne looked when he swaggered into a bar full of outlaws. Bart would start pressing against our knees with his head, lightly at first, and then not so lightly. Before we knew what was happening, he would shove us a couple of feet backward, grin, dance around for a minute, and then want his back rubbed more.

Even so, his actions were still kind of cute, but we knew we couldn't let him get away with it at 400 pounds because soon he would weigh 2,000 pounds and it wouldn't be so cute any more. So every time he started pushing against our knees we gave him a light rap on the nose with the heel of our boots. He quickly got to where every time he would see us begin to raise our foot, he would immediately stop pushing, uncock his head and his eyes would return to normal.

Now Bart is almost full-grown and every time we go out into the pasture to check the cows he comes running up to us to have his back scratched. It is always a little alarming at first to see a 2,000-pound animal running toward you. But even at his size, Bad Bart — the bull that can easily put three bulls that outweigh him by 200 pounds in their place and barrel through a barbed wire fence like it wasn't even there — still cringes at the sight of a raised boot.

After Bart finds out who his real father is, he will have to visit with Dr. Phil to find out why he recoils from a boot. "Is it any boot, Bart, or just the lizard skin Tony Lamas? Is this boot problem the truth you believe about yourself when no one else is looking? How's that working for you?"

56

The Tractor Road Less Traveled Leads To Dinner Out

ONE OF THE first things a rancher's wife learns is how to drive the tractor. So if you are a woman enamored with the idea of leading a home, home on the range lifestyle with long days of riding horses through cattle and antelope, and think you can obtain it by marrying a rancher, you better think twice. It's more like home, home, in the fields where the John Deere and the Massey Fergusons play.

I'm not saying that you don't get an opportunity to ride horses and work with the cattle, but that usually comes only after you've spent hours bouncing around in a tractor seat while plowing, disking, swathing, raking or baling hay, pulling a feed wagon or harrowing fields. And of course by then, with tractor tush setting in, you aren't too keen about getting on a horse anyway.

I recently had an opportunity to take my tractor driving to new heights of ecstasy. I had to drive it home from town where it had been in the shop for repairs. That doesn't sound like a big chore, but when you consider it takes the better part of a day to drive the 25-mile distance, it is both a mind and butt numbing experience.

When my husband dropped me off at the tractor shop for the drive home, I asked him if it had enough diesel in it.

"Yes, it has plenty," he said as he rolled his eyes at my inquiry.

"How do you know without checking," I said because the gas gauge hasn't worked on the tractor for several years.

"I know, it's fine," he said, "now stop fussing and hurry up so you can get home in time for dinner." Dinner? It was only 9 a.m., so now I was the one rolling my eyes.

"Maybe we can go out for dinner tonight?" I ventured...

thinking I'd be tired after spending so much of the day in the tractor.

"Nah, when I get home I'll take a roast out of the freezer for you to cook tonight," he said.

Rats!

Knowing that it would be a long journey, I had prepared for the tractor trip. I brought food and drinks, laptop computer, camera, cards for solitaire, blanket and pillow, extra change of clothes…

The first thing I discovered is that even though you are going unbelievably slow in a tractor down the highway, you can't type on a computer and drive at the same time. For one thing with such a bouncy seat, you can't keep the laptop on your lap. And the tractor won't steer itself. Oh, and you kind of have to watch where you are going, there's always that to contend with.

Unfortunately those little problems took care of any ideas of taking a nap too. And getting waved at with the middle finger three times in the first half-mile by people passing me in automobiles didn't give me much confidence in my ability to play solitaire while driving.

But, there was always the radio… And if I could actually have heard it over the sound of the tractor engine and the big wheels rotating on pavement, it would have been much easier to listen to.

I tried singing, but even I can't listen to myself for very long without wondering where that talent took a nosedive in my family's gene pool.

Along the way, I did however invent what I think would be a wonderful new video game called "Tractor Sideswipe." The idea is to see how many mailboxes you can hit with a tractor, or how many you can avoid. I decided to wait and see how well I did on my journey before committing to hitting the mailboxes or missing the mailboxes for the game.

I went through all of my food in the first three hours and was just about on my second bottle of water when a realization hit me. I'm not exactly pulling a porta-potty with me and there is no public bathroom for miles, actually none on my route unless you count the occasional large tree or abandoned barn. So I decided I better take it easy on the drinks.

Just about the time I was thinking it would be more fun to watch grass grow than drive a tractor home, the engine started to sputter. I pulled over to the side of the road as far as I could get, which means I was still covering most of one lane. The tractor died so I started it up again. It seemed to be running so I gave it some throttle and took off again.

About one quarter-mile down the road it started sputtering again so I pulled over a second time. This time it died and I couldn't get it started again. Fortunately I had my cell phone so I called my husband.

"What's wrong with it?" he asked.

"It died and won't start again," I replied.

He went through the usual check list… did you give it some throttle… did you turn off the choke after you got a little ways down the road… did you turn the key when you tried to start it… did you push in the clutch…

I replied an exasperated "yes" to all of the above.

A few minutes and about seven middle finger waves from passing motorists later, he arrived in his pickup and popped the hood and started checking things out. He fiddled with wires, pulled dipsticks out and tightened cables. I was still sitting in the tractor cab so he asked me to try starting it again.

It made a halfhearted attempt to engage the pistons and then died. My husband went around to the back of his pickup and emerged with a gas can full of diesel.

I swung open the door of the tractor cab and started to go into the I told you so routine, but thought better of it…

"Dinner out tonight?" I asked.

"I guess so," he said without looking up from pouring the diesel into the tank.

57

Caution, Driving with a Husband Is Hazardous

I LEARNED HOW to drive when I was about 13. My Dad took me out to a flat dirt field in the country in an older jeep and taught me how to shift gears without popping the clutch and killing the engine.

Later my mom taught me the finer art of parallel parking and maneuvering in traffic. Unfortunately, I had to figure out how to put on makeup in the rear-view mirror while driving on my own.

My brother, who is almost two years older, taught me how to peel out and spin cookies. (Oops! Sorry, I wasn't supposed to tell mom that!)

By the time I was in college, I was driving long distance road trips in all kinds of conditions including black ice, snow and fog, most of the time with a carload of noisy friends.

Nowadays I put about 20,000 miles a year in the driver's seat in our car, pickup, jeep and tractors combined. Sometimes I have to share my seat with the dog, but I think it's accurate to say I do most of the driving.

All of this isn't too unusual, but I had thought with this experience it would be safe to assume that I know how to drive. But apparently all of that early training and subsequent decades of driving is not sufficient, because my husband continues to give me instruction on an almost daily basis.

Several years ago when he decided that I should be the designated driver when we go places, I thought, "Wow, he must really think I'm a good driver!" Turns out he thought it would just be easier to tell me how to drive if he were in the passenger seat. Why he has decided to make it his primary goal in life to make me a better driver remains a mystery.

Even though I have been driving sticks for the better part of 30 years, and somehow manage to get where I am going without having the transmission fall out, apparently, according to him, I really don't know how to shift.

From his observations, he tells me I am either riding the clutch, holding it in too long, letting it out too fast or using the wrong part of my foot. I swear he must have a security camera on the floor by my left foot; otherwise, how can he see what's going on down there that well from the passenger seat? I just know that one of these days I'll be on the Internet at YouTube looking at funny cow videos and a video called "Debby Has Her Foot on the Clutch" will appear.

And then there is the stick itself. Apparently I operate it with all of the finesse of someone trying to cram a wet noodle through the eye of a needle. I should shift faster. I should shift slower. I should have shifted up when I shifted down, and down when I shifted up. I shift at the wrong time or I shift at the right time, and then it's back to the whole foot on the clutch thing.

He tells me to listen to the RPMs so I will know when to shift. I tell him to listen to the car door slam so he will know when I get out.

And this all takes place before I even get out of the driveway!

Once we're on the open road, I drive the speed limit and he says I drive too slow. He tells me I will get a ticket for impeding traffic, so I speed up. When he's not looking at the speedometer, I slow down again because I don't want to get a ticket for speeding.

With all of this speeding up and slowing down, I'm thinking of installing hazard warnings on my car — flashing yellow lights and a sign that reads "Caution, speed fluctuates due to nagging husband." Oops, sorry, he says he doesn't nag, he is just trying to help. "Caution, speed fluctuates due to husband trying to help."

Maybe I would be better off to get one of those window suction cup signs that says, "Husband on Board." That would probably clue most people in to what is going on.....

Once we get into town is when the real fun begins!

Apparently I wait too long for cars to pass before I pull out into the street. After all if we could have trimmed three seconds off of that wait, we'd get home three seconds sooner.

He also says I'm always taking corners too close or too fast. Most women get excited if they get a new job with a big fat raise, someone gives them diamonds or they have a baby. If I could turn a corner at the right angle and velocity it would be right up there with that kind of thrill.

Backing up and parallel parking – let's not even go there! Many married couples have divorced over far less strenuous situations.

And parking lots are like kryptonite to Superman — they are best avoided. Some day I should get the Nobel Peace Prize for finding the right place to park in a parking lot — that is if I ever do.

Traffic lights, stop signs and pedestrians are always getting in our way of making good time. Making good time appears to be right at the top of the list of important things to accomplish, just above saving the planet.

Either I stop at the lights or for pedestrians for too long, or don't even need to stop in the first place. I'm wondering if we could call the local police and have them clear the way for us when we come to town.

"Yes, this is Debby Schoeningh, I'm coming to town with my husband. Can you please time it so all of the lights are green when we go through and not allow anyone to cross the street during our visit? Also, please notify all available units that we need to make good time."

Police dispatch would immediately radio their officers, "Schoeningh is coming to town again and she has her husband with her. If you want that Christmas bonus you better make sure they are in and out of town in less than 30 minutes. And disregard any traffic violations; her husband is still teaching her how to drive."

When the Department of Motor Vehicles teach about driving hazards, they forget to mention the dangers of having your husband with you....

"What?" Hang on a second; my husband is looking over my shoulder as I write this. He says he thinks I may be exaggerating.

"Well, maybe I am, a little…."

Follow the Author

Website: https://www.thecountrysidepress.com

Facebook: https://www.facebook.com/thecountrysidepress

See Other Books by Debby Schoeningh

Amazon: https://www.amazon.com/author/debbyschoeningh

Debby lives one chapter at a time in rural Oregon where she finds humor in every day life on the ranch with her husband and two wiener dogs. Debby mostly laughs at herself, except cows, she laughs at cows. Cows are funny and don't seem to mind being laughed at. Cows are mostly irritated by her presence.

Made in the USA
Monee, IL
11 August 2022